FROM THE SHADOWS OF MY SOUL

STEVEN W. WISE

ABOUT THE AUTHOR

Steven W. Wise, a graduate of the University of Missouri, is a licensed real estate appraiser. He lives and writes his stories on a wooded farm near Columbia, Missouri, with his wife, Cathy. Published novels include *Chimborazo, Midnight, Chambers, Long Train Passing,* and *The Jordan Tracks.*

The serpent was the smartest creature in the Garden of Eden, but his competition didn't amount to much. Still doesn't.

The only perfect thing is the imperfection of man.

CONTENTS

In 1918, when my beloved grandfather was eighteen, he saved up in a cigar box enough money to purchase his first suit of clothes. His father somehow found out about it and one Saturday afternoon emptied the box, took the money to the local tavern, and proceeded with his bar mates to drink up every cent. My father told me the story many years after we buried Gramps, and he told me that many years passed after the incident before Gramps owned his first suit. Sometimes, hauntings are passed down through the generations— heirlooms of sorrow.

NOBODY BUT THE DIGGER

He kept his treasure stored in a cigar box hidden in the back of a drawer, and in the end, it was the joining of the sun with the silver stored inside, and the grunts of hogs, that would cause the boy to stand over his father with a crowbar in his hands as the soft cherry light of the next dawn seeped into the bedroom. But now it was late-afternoon on the first Saturday in March of 1918, and the wind was a razor on his face as he stood transfixed before the tall glass window of Heck's General Store. The sharpness found the holes in his homespun trousers and curled inside his flapping coat held together by a single remaining button. From behind him, the mare whinnied from the wagon harness. He paid no mind to the mare or the wind. The suit beyond the glass was crafted in wool and black in color, but not the dead black that attracted no notice; rather, a black that somehow sucked the slanting rays of sunlight deep into the fibers and enriched them, gave them back to his eyes as a mysterious hue: nameless, dreamy, perfect. Pinned to the right sleeve was a rectangular price tag that read: $18.50. Virgil Barrow was a month from his seventeenth birthday, and although he could not mark the exact date, he reckoned that he had begun saving for his first suit of clothes nearly two years ago. Stanley Heck and his wife could afford to inventory only one quality suit for sale in their store, so Virgil had studied more than a dozen as the months piled up along with his treasure. They came and they went—all pleasing in their own way—but the one he stared at now was the finest, he was certain.

The tall door creaked and Stanley Heck's visor-covered head appeared in the manner of a squirrel poking its head from a hole in a tree. "We're not closing for ten minutes, son. Want to come inside and see it again?"

"I reckon not, Mr. Heck. Got to get the wagon back for Pa."

Heck nodded, scrunched his features without realizing it, then said, "Saturday night at Wiley's Tavern. I understand."

Virgil shifted his weight, did not reply, looked back at the suit.

"Well, it'll be yours soon anyhow, and you can do a sight more than stare at it. The wife will fit it to you like it was made for you to start with, I guarantee. Besides, looks close to your fit as it is."

The boy smiled, said, "Yes sir." He held his right thumb and forefinger a quarter- inch apart.

"How close does that mean, Virgil?"

"It means sixty-seven cents." He smiled again, wider than before, but his lips remained sealed. He raised a hand in a parting gesture as he turned away.

Heck closed the door and walked back to the counter, where his wife was thumbing through a small stack of sales slips. She glanced up, shook her head slowly, then said, "It always pains me to see that boy. Living out there with that no-account Lank Barrow, scratchin' in the dirt on that sorry mess of a pig farm...mother and brother long in their graves... Lordy."

"That's just the way it works out sometimes. Some boys have to be men too early...never were children. He's one of those." He shrugged his shoulders. "But then again, he could be scratchin' in the dirt with General Pershing's boys fightin' the Hun in France if he'd been born a couple years sooner."

The woman huffed. "Not a wide difference, you ask me."

Virgil bounced on the wagon seat as the mare negotiated the rutted road leading to the house and the tall man standing ramrod straight on the small stoop leading to the front door. Lank Barrow's great hands hung from the sleeve of his best coat like tools at rest, thick fingers half curled, ready to open or finish the curl into a fist as the need arose. Under the coat he wore a clean white cotton shirt with black buttons, tweed trousers, and on his feet were low-heeled work boots. He was a man of long lines—from the top: forehead, nose, jaw line, neck—all linked to corded arms and sloped shoulders that tapered to a waist that had remained the same since he was the age of his son. His eyes were sea green, deep set under black brows, as untamed as the hair that spilled from under his bowler hat. Sometime during the past year, both father and son had come to the realization that looking at one another was like looking into a mirror—the past for Lank, the future for Virgil—but neither would ever speak of it, despite the certainty that the images had appeared.

Virgil reined in, looked at his father, waited.

"Quarter hour more and your ass woulda been in a fix."

The boy looked down at the floorboard. "Yes sir, I know. But I'm here now."

"You get her watered, then get the bag on her while you unload. I aim to head back to town right soon."

"I will."

Fifteen minutes later, Virgil parked the freshened mare and the empty wagon in front of the house. Inside, he walked to the kitchen and pumped water for washing his hands and then filled a tin cup, drank it. His stomach growled with emptiness and he looked at the cupboard shelf, saw a ham bone with plenty of meat remaining that would do for supper after his father had departed. He shuffled into his bedroom and plopped down on the edge of his bed, leaned back and stuck his hand into his pocket, felt for the three dimes. Then he waited for the blessed sounds of departure. First came the heavy clomp of boots, then the front door opening, quickly followed by the slamming. Virgil stood, rubbed the three coins together in his fingers, his mind now locked on the top drawer of his old dresser and the cigar box stuffed behind a wad of long underwear. The commotion that the big sow was raising in the hog lot came only to the edge of his hearing and he dismissed it as he stood and walked to the dresser.

Outside, from the wagon seat, Lank heard the grunts and squeals, but did not dismiss them as inconsequential. The old sow had a mean streak, but she was his best producer and he had to put up with it until that sweet day when she wasn't, and he could put a .22 bullet squarely between her beady eyes and turn her into meat.

He threw down the reigns, and hopped off the wagon seat. "You ornery old bitch of a hag!" He stomped around the corner of the house, but had no intention of dealing with the pen and stinking up his good boots with pig shit

4

on a Saturday night. He headed for the window to Virgil's bedroom and looked in, his knuckles cocked and ready to rap on the glass that filtered the last of the sunlight and directed it toward the shiny objects that the boy was tossing in his palm. Lank slowly lowered his hand and peered with hawk's eyes past the boy's shoulder, identified the objects as silver coins. He watched his son drop them into a box, and then stir and poke at the contents with his fingertips.

Lank strode to the front door, opened it quickly, and walked directly to the boy's bedroom. Virgil was standing with the dresser at his back, both hands empty, fingers clutched into loose fists.

Lank nodded at the dresser, said, "And just what the hell is that all about?"

Virgil swallowed, sucked a quick breath in through his nose. "What do you mean...that?"

"Boy, don't play games with me." Lank took a step forward and brushed Virgil aside with a swipe of his forearm and opened the top dresser drawer. Within seconds he found the box, cradled it in his right hand. He opened the lid, looked inside. "Well now, no wonder you was hidin' this from me."

"I...I wasn't hidin' nothin', Pa. I been savin' for a long time."

Lank sneered, said, "Savin'...what the hell you need to be savin' for? I work my ass off around here so you can have what you need, and I find out you been squirrelin' this kind of money away."

"I been...thinkin' about a suit of clothes...down to Heck's store."

Lank huffed a mirthless laugh. "A suit? That's the damndest idea I ever heard of, boy. You need a suit 'bout as bad as one of them young shoats in the pen. You got hand-medowns in plenty good shape, and prob'ly a decent coat and britches in the attic if you wasn't too lazy to go look."

"Pa, I worked that job money up in town without ever lettin' up a lick out here...mostly on Sunday mornings at near about every place you can name."

Lank stared his son down, waited until the boy lowered his head. He turned the box sideways, shook part of the coins into his right hand, then into his coat pocket. He repeated the process two more times, and then banged the empty box on the dresser top. He turned and walked away.

When Lank reached the wagon seat, the door opened and Virgil stepped outside. "Pa, I'm askin' you proper...like a man to a man. Don't do this to me."

Lank felt his face flush hot and red. He turned, dropped the reigns, and swung one leg from the seat before he froze in place at the sight of his son. Virgil's eyes were searing, his tall form rigid, tight fists formed like cudgels hanging from his arms. Hard words formed inside of Lank's head and made their way to his half-opened mouth, but he said only, "Well I'll be goddamned."

He reset himself on the seat, picked up the reigns and flicked the mare's back. Virgil trotted behind the wagon for a few seconds, then stopped, shouted, "Look back here, Pa! I'm beggin' you!"

Lank popped the reigns and the wagon creaked and groaned as it sped down the rutted lane.

Virgil laid on his bed fully clothed, his boots laced tight. His hands were joined and resting squarely on the center of his chest. The time of parting—cold and set in the stone of forever—drew near. The tears had dried into stiff crooked lines high on his cheeks, the longings now dried and stiff too, like the buried bones of his mother and brother. The night chill seeped in through the walls and settled about him. On the floor beside the door was a rucksack containing his best coveralls, two sets of long underwear, two woolen shirts, three pairs of socks, three days worth of food wrapped in a dirty oilcloth, a tin cup, and ten feet of coiled hemp rope. On the rucksack rested a wide-brimmed hat. In his coat pockets were a bone-handled knife in a leather sheath, a flint rock, two dozen Diamond matches in a small glass jar with a tight lid, a small tablet of paper, two pencils, and a copy of *The Tale of Peter Rabbit* that had no front cover. His trouser pockets were empty. Resting against the door jamb was a six-foot crowbar.

He reckoned it was two hours past midnight when the distant rumble of wagon wheels leaked into his room. He listened intently as the sounds grew louder and then ceased in front of the house. The mare snorted a complaint about the poor habits of her master and then fell silent. Virgil felt the vibrations from the slamming of the door, and then heavy, uneven footfalls pounded toward Lank's bedroom. First one boot clumped to the floor and then the other, followed by slurred notes from an unrecognizable tune, and the creak of bedsprings, and finally silence, save for the night wind pushing around the corner of the house. Virgil closed his eyes, but did not sleep.

The first hint of dawn was only a softening of the blackness, but some dawns hurry, and the gray light came like smoke filling the room, and soon Virgil's eyes blinked in the flushed hue from sunlight filtered through a bank of clouds in the eastern sky. His chest rose with a deep inhalation and he exhaled as slowly as he could, gathering himself for the cruel minutes to come and the unknown world beyond the minutes. He pushed up from the bed, waited for the blood to rearrange, give him back his arms and legs. He walked to the door, pulled it open, and then lifted his hat and rucksack with his left hand and the crowbar with his right. He placed the hat and rucksack on the floor beside the front door, turned back and entered the open door to his father's bedroom. He leaned the crowbar against the wall. The man was a tangle of quilts and arms and legs askew, the air curdled and stagnant. On the floor beside the bed were his outer garments, and Virgil picked up the trousers, ran his hand into an empty pocket. He fished inside the other pocket and pulled out two dimes, a nickel, and five pennies. These he slid into his own pocket. He reached for the crowbar, and poked the end hard against a quilt-covered shin. The leg recoiled involuntarily, and a loud groan arose from Lank's chest. The long face, framed by wild black hair, popped up from the quilt, and stunned, blinking eyes sought the source of the pain. He looked down at his throbbing leg and clamped a hand over it, as if to confirm that he was not dreaming. Then he looked up, saw his son two steps away, the crowbar held in both hands and resting on his right shoulder.

"Wh…What the…"

"Shut up, pa, don't say a word."

Lank swiped a hand over his face, pointed a finger. "Listen, boy…"

Virgil raised the bar from his shoulder, coiled his arms. "Shut up! Or I swear I'll start with this bar and that bed will look like we butchered on it 'fore I stop."

Lank raised himself to a sitting position and slowly pushed back toward the headboard, which banged against the wall when his back hit it.

Virgil took a step toward the bed, and then lowered the bar to his shoulder. "I got things to say before I leave, and all you're gonna do is listen. I've worked and done the best I could since I was little. I never once whined or thought

8

pity on myself. I lost out on the schoolin' and can't half read or write, and I'm bad shamed by that. And I took the whippins and the cussin' and just kept on, thinkin' that one day you'd come to see me as a man and let me stand alongside you. After I knew it wasn't your nature to love, I set that away too, and just waited to be your friend...that would've been enough. For near two years, I've been more man than boy in every way there is, but still, I waited...hoped."

Virgil closed his eyes for a second, looked up, blinked against the wetness. "But I went to thinkin' while you were at the tavern, and on through the night...and I know that it can never be right between me and you. If it hadn't been the suit money, it woulda' been somethin' else that made me know for sure." He paused, shook his head. "I was all you had in this world, but now I'm gonna walk out that door and never look back and walk straight west past the Smokies into some kind of life fit for a man." He wept now, did not care, let the snot stream from his nose to mingle with the tears. "Damn you! I would have sat grandbabies on your knee to help your hard-ass heart...and I would have looked after you when you were old...but now, one day your heart will give out, or you'll fall drunk from the wagon and hit your head, or a bad sow will get you down in the pen...and then the county will have to sell you out just to bury you, and there won't be nobody at the grave but the digger."

The labored sounds of breathing filled the room, made it seem like a box to both father and son. Virgil raised the bar and with a great cry lunged toward the bed and swung it in a wide arc. The iron tore through the headboard like a knife through bread and when it stopped, a foot of its length had disappeared beyond the wall of the house. Lank had not moved a muscle, knew that if his son had aimed to kill him there would have been no escape.

Virgil swiped his coat sleeve across his face, pointed a finger at Lank. "I leave you with this: one day, when my little ones are old enough to wonder, and they ask me about my own father, I'm gonna tell 'em I was raised in a orphan home, and that I never knew you." He turned away, walked to the doorway, turned back. "One time, I heard a man who didn't believe in God say there weren't no heaven or hell, and that he figured when he died, he'd feel just like he did before he was born. God, if he is out there, ain't seen fit to treat me kind so far, but I'm gonna give him another chance across the mountains. I ain't yet bought all the way into what the man said, but I do allow that is the best *you* can ever hope for."

He spun away from the bed and quickly gathered his provisions, jammed his hat on his head, flung open the door. When he was twenty steps down the lane, Virgil heard his father run toward him, but he kept walking.

"Boy!...son!...son!, stop...listen!"

Virgil shook his head, picked up his pace.

"Look back here, Virgil...I'm down on my knees...I'm beggin' you...please!"

Virgil stopped, made only a quarter turn, did not look back. He raised his right arm, swung it behind him with a balled fist at the end. "You come after me, I will kill you."

On Monday morning, Stanley Heck, visor in place and broom in hand, unlocked the front door to his store and stepped out onto the boardwalk. The piece of paper floated down and came to rest near the toes of his boots. He picked it up and unfolded it, slipped his spectacles from his vest pocket and set them in place.

To Mr Heck I do not wont th sut anymor. I am sory godby Virgil

Stanley went back inside the store, walked to the counter and laid the note in front of his wife. She read it, shook her head, said, "Something's bad wrong about this, Stanley, and I don't like it one little bit."

He nodded, said, "We're in agreement on that account, Hazel."

"Well, I intend to find the sheriff and tell him to go out there and see about that boy." She reached behind her to untie her apron.

Stanley waved a hand at her, shook his head. "No, you're not going to do that. It's not necessary."

"And just how do you reach that conclusion, sir?"

He walked slowly to the window and stood behind the black suit, looked past it and through the glass at the sagging awning above the front door to Wiley's Tavern. He said, "It's not necessary because, one way or the other, they settled it between them. And if what happened out there is what I think might have happened, then I want him to have all the head start he can get."

He returned to the counter, picked up the note, and walked to the black wood stove squatting in the middle of the store. He tore the note into small pieces before opening the door and tossing them inside.

"Are you all right with that, Mrs. Heck?"

"Indeed, I am."

I have read about and studied the details of hundreds of battles, ranging from the Revolutionary War to the present. Many have found permanent places within the storage compartments of my grey matter, but none more securely tucked away than this true story from The Somme. The logistical details are as accurate as a reading of history will allow, including the final body count. I created four characters to hopefully bring to life the heart-rending story of this useless spillage of blood. I believe in the power of voices from beyond the grave—perhaps the only location from which a voice has no reason to tell lies.

MACHINE GUN AT THE CRUCIFIX

The Tribes of Earth

Can it be fancied that God ever vindictively made in his image a mannequin merely to madden it?

Edgar Allan Poe

On the morning of 1 July 1916, sunlight crept over the crest of a ridge, nudging the shadows from the expanse of trees known as Mansell Copse. One kilometer to the west, the town of Mametz—its inhabitants shuffling awake in dread of a war morning—carved a modest acreage from the French countryside. At the foot of a hill rising to Mansell Copse, one hundred and sixty men who were a component of the 8th and 9th Battalions of the British Devonshire Regiment leaned against the dank earth of their section of trench.

"Tis a beauty of a morning, eh, lads?" The silky baritone belied the fact that Noel Torrance had lived for little more than nineteen years and had left Cambridge University to fight the Germans. But his features did not belie his age: cheekbones carved high, framing a nose almost too perfect, liquid green eyes that hid nothing. Pinched in the corner of his mouth was a cigarette of Turkish origin, its white paper skin an angled line of contrast against the backdrop of filthy cheek. The man on his left ignored him, preferring to hum tunelessly into the clumps of chalky soil a few inches from his nose.

"That it would be, Noel...though I can think of a great many preferred locations from which to see it," replied the man pressed against his right shoulder. Cecil Coalthorpe stood a half foot taller than Torrance, but the top of his helmet was even with his comrade's. They had all quickly learned that standing to one's full height was not a good habit on the battlefield, and Coalthorpe had stooped for so long that the comma of his spine now appeared quite natural. His face was the fleshy antithesis of his best friend's, marked by a crooked smile that exposed a pronounced overbite. A shock of unruly hair jutted like sand colored weeds from the front of his helmet. Nonetheless, he exuded the winsomeness of a young man who had no need for the prop of handsome features.

With two fingers, Torrance centered the cigarette in his lips, then sucked the smoke deeply into his lungs, waiting for the strong tobacco to register its little brain whirl beneath the bone of his forehead before releasing the gray cloud. The foreboding—a small, pure mass with its own center of gravity—

grew alongside the whirl, but for at least a few minutes more he knew that he would be able to support the weight without assistance. "Damned I am if anybody makes a better cigarette than the Turks."

The five men of the German machine gun crew huddled near the stone shrine guarding the cemetery at the southern edge of Mametz. The structure was three meters square at the base, standing twice the height of the men, and atop it, rising three meters more, rested a crucifix. Before them stretched a shallow valley, bereft of a single tree, and though none of them had given voice to it, they all believed that the chances of British troops attempting a direct advance over the naked four-hundred-meter expanse were remote. Still, the German crew members were well prepared, believing that they at least would have distant targets of opportunity at the flank of any charging men.

The gunner, a bear-like man named Werner Gruber, sat with his back pressed into the carved stone wall of the shrine, storing in his body the delightful coolness. He possessed a slope-shouldered strength that had caused many in his regiment to wonder aloud—in only partial jest—why a full crew of four assistants trailed him around the countryside, given that he appeared to be singularly capable of lugging the gun and its sledge with no more effort than an ordinary man carrying a basket of peaches. His proficiency with the gun had grown to near legendary proportion, and, in fact, the lofty status had been well earned.

The preparations had been complete for more than a half hour, each man having performed the routine tasks with neither thoughts nor words required. Gruber rotated his head, peered inside the shrine at Maschinengewehr 08, the metal brute squatting in dark menace from its sledge. From the flank of the beast hung a 250-round fabric belt that would soon feed it, the empty casings passing out the opposite flank after spitting their 7.92mm bullets down the water-cooled barrel. The square-faced man swept his vision over the 400 meters of shadowed valley, a mirthless smile creasing his face as he remembered occasions on which he had cut men down from 1,500 meters. Twenty-nine more belts were boxed neatly at the ready.

Gruber studied the black half-moons of grime sealed under the fingernails of his right hand for several seconds before running the thick fingers through matted, light brown hair. He pinched his eyes into slits, cast his gaze in a slow sweep over the valley, from left to right—as was his habit with the gun—imprinting his brain with the subtle rises and depressions. Soon, ghost images of men floated along the undulating landscape, hunched over the way they always were—helmeted heads tucked into their shoulders, as if running into a wind-blown sheet of rain. He watched the ghost men lurching toward him, stumbling as they struggled to find footholds in the ragged earth, wondered how many men he would transform into ghosts within the hour. He blinked them away.

A low rumble leaked from his chest, then he said to the man nearest him, "Perhaps they will, Stefan, after all, charge up this slope toward the Christ image, believing it might give them strength against our gun."

Stefan Hinkel, his boyish features round and clumped about a scraggly blond moustache in the center of his face, huffed against the idea. He craned his head upward and over his shoulder, tossed a glance toward the crucifix, then said, "Naaa...the hanging man does not look like he could bolster the courage of soldiers."

"But to many, he is not just a *man*, Stefan. He is the Christ...and this," he raised his arm, "his image. It is a powerful image."

"To some."

Gruber allowed the silence to thicken, could wait no longer for the ridding of the burden. "I am thankful that it was not my decision to set up in this place."

Hinkel shook his head slowly, said, "And after all that has happened...all of the friends we have left slaughtered, unburied in the mud...all of the enemy we have killed and maimed...after all of this, you still believe in...that." He gestured wearily with a flap of his right arm.

"I cling. I do not wish to let it go."

"Let it go. There is no god who would preside over this war."

"I do not believe He...presides...over it, as you say."

"But if he were God all mighty, he would be *allowing* it." He pointed toward the valley, mimicked the stutter of the machine gun. "There is no difference."

Hinkel watched as Gruber lowered his massive head, and with his right thumb trace a long line in the bare soil. Then, with his left thumb, he formed the high beam of his earthen cross.

Hinkel said, "Ah...the master gunner behind Maschinengewehr 08...look at you. Why can't you see?"

"See what?"

"You use your thumbs to make your little dirt cross. The same thumbs that will trip the trigger of our gun if they are stupid enough to attack toward their crucified man." He smiled ruefully, said, "No true god would allow you...or any of us...or any of them... to be the killer of many men for the trading of fucking muddy slits in French ground crawling with rats and littered with rotting bodies!"

The other crew members faded into the shadows, had no wish to be drawn into the brewing thing that had dogged the two men for weeks.

"No...no...there is more to it than that—the killing—I tell you." Gruber said. "We fight for our country, a cause."

Hinkel clamped his mouth shut, felt the pressure in his jaws as his teeth clenched in opposition. He closed his eyes, relaxed his jaw muscles, found the exquisite treasure chest in the center of his brain. In the coffer were paintings indelibly imprinted, and the man sifted through them lovingly as he drank in the late spring aroma of thick fir and spruce that covered his Black Forest homestead. A white, crushed rock path cut a tiny, rising seam through greenery so dense and dark that it was indeed black. But it was not a foreboding black; he had never believed in the old forest legends and fairy tales dribbling from the thin lips of old men and women. The wind stirred and swept down the path on which he again walked, and Stefan Hinkel believed that he was as close to paradise as a man could be. He held the painting, allowed himself to be suspended in time and space, saw the forest and smelled the green and black perfume and felt the breeze on his face and studied the splendor of the treetops as they reached like a sea of fingers beseeching the blue sky—a vast, sweeping moment when the purity of it all once again tempted him to seek the god of Werner Gruber. But then came the creak of the treasure chest lid, and after it fastened securely, Hinkel knew that the red place would come and fill the void. Involuntarily, his jaw muscles again tightened, and he opened his eyes.

"You are an idealist, Werner...a foolish dreamer...of God and Christ and paradise. You have tramped through shit and blood and broken men and dead men for twenty months now...and soon, when the beautiful morning sun lights this valley for you...this valley of the crucifix...of your hanging god...you will use the light and the gun to open bellies like a butcher with his clever and make more shit and blood and broken and dead men!"

He was spent now, did not care that he had finally punched through the flimsy wall that guarded a tenuous comradeship, nor could he identify precisely the chamber of his brain from which the words spewed. The red place in his head had festered and grown over the course of hundreds of nights lost in the venue of nightmares at the edge of sleep— nightmares with boundaries sealed by the staccato chatter of death from Maschinengewehr 08, with a man at the trigger who claimed God. He slumped forward, curled his arms around his knees, said evenly, "All of us...nothing more than warring, godless tribes...the tribes of earth." A long sigh seeped from his chest. "And I don't want this pissy little town of Mametz any more than the British want my homestead." He paused, pointed his forefinger at the machine gun. "Just kill them, master gunner Werner Gruber. I don't really give a damn if you let it go or not. Just kill them all if you can. I want to go home...to see the Black Forest again."

Noel Torrance fished a cigarette from the crumpled pack, then lit it carefully after waiting for the acrid smell of sulfur from the match flame to dissipate. The familiar ripple that always foretold the blowing of whistles loomed; he hoped that he would not have to hurry his smoking, or the voicing of thoughts now finalized. The hurrying would come soon enough.

He flicked the tip of his tongue at a particle of tobacco on his upper lip, then said, "Word is that our good Captain Duncan Martin has studied the contour maps for the lay of the land up there, and has opined rather strongly that if we advance we will be in a spot of trouble."

Coalthorpe nodded, said, "So I've heard, but what of it? The whole of France is rather a spot of trouble, seems to me."

"Ummm...I believe that this particular spot may prove noteworthy indeed."

Coalthorpe arched his eyebrows dramatically. "And you, military expert not twenty years off his mum's teat...how is it that you've been granted such omniscience?"

"It's Captain Martin. He hasn't been himself since he came back from leave, and that's where they say he studied the maps...even fashioned a model of the ground to show to his superiors."

"Ahhh...some lads return from short ruts with their ladies in good sorts...others not. He's probably just one of the others."

Torrance slowly shook his head. "I've been within a few steps of him several times, last night and this morning. Before, there was always something about him...a sturdier Devonshire man I had never seen, the bearing...the force of him, as if I could see the energy oozing from his features. But now..." His voice trailed away.

"So your youthful omniscience extends into the mind and heart of our captain, does it now, Noel." He huffed a laugh. "I tell you, he was denied his furry pokings back home, or some such."

Torrance refused the offer of banter, allowed his cigarette to form a quarter inch of ash as he stared into the distance beyond the rim of the trench. He flicked the ash, drew in a precise measure of smoke, then said, "I am but a youth in years, true enough, but the last months have shown me much, and much of that, things I did not wish to be shown." The cigarette slipped from his fingers onto his boot top. "And what I saw in his face...I did not wish to be shown."

Coalthorpe said, "Look at me, my friend. You have seen my face since we were boys. What do you see now?"

"I don't even need to see your face, Cecil. I know what I would see."

"And…?"

"The brave face of a Devonshire…but one who whistles in the cemetery…like all of us."

"And the whistling, is it such a bad thing?"

"The generals approve, I'm sure. It helps us to go over the top."

Coalthorpe swallowed, looked into the birth of morning—sunlight burning away the edges of retreating gloom, the freshening waves of long grass sprinkled with wildflowers rising ever upward toward the emerald offerings of Mansell Copse—these things and more the man looked at, but did not see.

"Goddamn the generals, from Haig on down," Torrance said softly.

Coalthorpe felt the blasphemy scratch his soul; never before had he heard such a curse escape the mouth of his friend—or his own mouth—their common vulgarities always devoid of references to Deity. Yet the scratch faded; the harsh word seemed fitting as it hung in the air between them.

"One!" Torrance's forefinger sprang from his fist and he jammed it into his chest. "Two!" He raised two fingers, stabbed them against Coalthorpe's chest. "It would make equal sense if our goddamned general just walked down our line, first numbering us…one by two…one by two…and then came back down the line with a small firing squad and ordered it to shoot the 'ones'…or the 'twos'…whichever number suited him. Then he could send a runner up to Mametz to tell their goddamned general that they could have the bloody town, and that the live half of us were going home."

"Along with him of course."

"Of course. At least his written memoirs would actually be truthful, as well as entertaining. But we will go about it the regular way, and he will write of the courage of his fallen men, instead of their forced insanity...which I now believe to be no different than courage."

Coalthorpe said, "If the land lies as Martin believes, why would they not site a machine gun up high?"

"Oh they have, Cecil, believe me. German Army standard issue MG 08, it is. And if the Bosch gunner is worth his salt, and if his crew is good, and they keep the gun running for the time it takes us to eat the meat and cheese from our rations...well then...it will be worse than just the half dying."

Coalthorpe raised his head to the sky. "Worse, you say?"

"Much worse."

Coalthorpe glanced past Torrance at the humming man, who had not moved a muscle for ten minutes. "Maybe Higgins there has it figured out after all...just lightly hum a nothing tune like a lunatic until we go for our little jaunt... just stay quiet."

Torrance stared straight ahead, and Coalthorpe knew that his friend would speak no more while they remained in the trench. He wondered if he would ever again hear him speak. Coalthorpe said, "Naaa...quiet doesn't fit me just now."

The words to come crowded on his tongue, and for a few seconds, the fleeting, sad image of his mother's visage materialized. He waited for the image to fade—knew that it must before he would be able to spill the words—then said, "I goddamn the generals too...from Haig on down."

The first whistle shriek, soon followed by many more, split the silence of morning, and in the instant before the scramble for the top, the line rippled with the internal buzz of men.

With elbows and knees and toes of boots, the Devonshires churned up from the trench—helmeted, heavy-laden worker ants serving their queen—and formed a loosely serrated line one hundred and sixty men in length. Noel Torrance, Cecil Coalthorpe, and the humming Higgins were squarely in the middle. At first sheltered by the grassy brow of the ridge and the trees of Mansell Copse, the line advanced steadily to the far edge of no man's land.

With rising dread, Torrance registered in the soles of his feet the level ground of the ridge top. Too soon, as the rhythmic whip of boots in long grass rose in his ears, the measured descent into the exposed valley sprawled before him. His brain whirred with distances—ever decreasing bands of separation: one hundred meters until they crossed the main road cutting through the valley floor, then up again, four hundred more—and when Noel Torrance finally dared to squint upward through the slash of sunlight, he spied the stone cross atop the shrine—a symbol both far and near—and felt the warm, blessed tingle of hope chase up his backbone.

Oh thou, Christ, hanging high on the hill...sweet Christ... deliver us from evil...let not this be our Golgotha...

The hard-packed road passed swiftly beneath him, but now the sound of boots in long grass was a roar, and with the roar came the mournful chatter of the German machine gun. Then Higgins, whose humming had ceased, pressed against his left shoulder, and Torrance cast a sidelong glance, saw tears spilling down his cheeks, smelled the stench from the man's bowels.

Torrance said, conversationally it seemed to Coalthorpe— like a mundane proclamation from a weary politician: "Higgins shit himself."

Coalthorpe replied, "Appropriate enough, that."

The first cries from the dying arose far to the right of the three men, cascading toward them before ceasing, as did the sound of the gun. Within seconds, the gun erupted anew, and the wails and groans came to them from the far left.

A sergeant named Thresher, standing to his full height and pointing at the distant cross, shouted, "The cross! He's under the cross...in the shrine! Don't let him bunch us in the middle! Advance and disperse!"

From the corner of his eye, Torrance saw Coalthorpe careening up the slope to his right, and he followed him, felt the steel bands of Higgins' fingers clutching his upper arm. They side-stepped two bodies, one draped atop the other, forming a precise "X." They ran past a man sitting squarely in the grass, staring at his shredded right hand as if studying an intriguing, red object on display in an art gallery. The machine-gunner was sweeping the middle of the line now with controlled, professional bursts, and Torrance knew that this German was the Grim Reaper come to life, the bullets from his gun a scythe harvesting men. On they ran, men possessed, through a lethal, whirling world.

Like hail swirling at the edge of a thunderstorm, the hiss and zip of bullets grew louder, chasing the three men as they stumbled into a shallow gulley. As one, three distinct sounds—a wet thud, the quick buzz of a wasp in his right ear, and a grunt— registered from left to right in Torrance's brain, and after they crashed to the ground, he sorted out the noises. Higgins was sprawled on his back, head tilted toward Torrance, who at first could see nothing amiss, and then realized that one eye had been replaced with a black hole. He quickly rolled over to Coalthorpe, who was tearing at his uniform top with his left hand.

Torrance brushed away his friend's hand, completed the task, and then peered closely at the wound. "Move your arm...can you move your arm?"

Coalthorpe raised his elbow cautiously at first, then slowly flapped it twice. "Yes...yes...it works."

Torrance used the torn uniform to dab at the blood, of which there was very little. "It's nothing, Cecil...just cut a little crease in your armpit."

"It does burn a bit." He looked past Torrance. "Higgins?"

"Finished...head."

Coalthorpe looked to his right, saw a rail-thin man they all called Stilts lying on his side, probing carefully with his fingers at the whitish shard of jawbone angling from his head. Coalthorpe attempted to swallow, could not. He turned back to Torrance, said, "We should say something."

Torrance looked down, shook his head. "Don't want to."

Coalthorpe said, "Mum said it was the whiskey saved me...little drops...when I was a week old...pneumonia. She said I was spared for a reason." He snapped his eyelids at the tears, swept his left hand toward the killing field. "For this?"

Torrance covered his helmet with his hands, rocked his head and shoulders side to side. "Be quiet, Cecil...please... just be quiet."

They sucked in air, listened to the hammer of the gun, but could not hear the hiss of bullets. Then the stern voice of Captain Martin rolled toward them. He was standing, thirty meters away, shaking his right fist like a man pounding a lectern. "Advance! Advance on the right! When the gun sweeps left, we must advance! There is only one gun up there!"

Torrance snatched his rifle from the grass, said to Coalthorpe, "If we can flank the bastard and get inside of fifty meters...only chance." He began to run, his chest brushing the grass tops, and Coalthorpe followed him.

Torrance opened his mouth, gulped the air with great heaves of his chest, ran until his legs refused another step, then flopped face-down into a barren patch of earth. He tilted up the rim of his helmet, saw the stone crucifix— immense and pale—saw the tops of German helmets in the nest, the smoke rising from the muzzle of MG 08.

Coalthorpe clamped a hand on Torrance's shoulder, then said, "Look. Martin has the bombing party within seventy-five meters."

Torrance looked at their only chance of salvation, noted that the full crew of nine had been reduced to four—two carriers, each lugging a green canvas bag of Mills bombs, and two throwers, with useless rifles already cast aside. Martin, armed only with the revolver in his right hand, ran three paces in front. Torrance looked past Martin and his brave band, searched desperately for other advancing Devonshires, saw only the crumpled, still shapes of men strewn over the field.

Oh, thou Christ…hanging so near…deliver us from evil…

Torrance said, "We can't stop, Cecil…have to get closer… get some bullets zinging round their heads at least."

With tortured muscle and tendon and bone, with spittle and snot spraying their cheeks and gaping mouths, the two young men got up and stumbled forward for only a few steps; they could run no more. They slammed to the ground on their knees, catching part of their weight with rifle butts. The hiss and zip grew louder.

Deliver us…

"Shoot, Cecil! Shoot now!"

They raised their rifles, muzzles wavering, and squeezed the triggers and worked the bolts as fast as they could. Neither man heard the cries and grunts of death arising from Martin and his men. Nor did they hear the sounds escaping their own bodies as the bullets tore through them. For long, strangely peaceful moments, they were aware only of being transformed—somehow placed on the ground by forces beyond comprehension—uncertain if they were still a part of life.

Torrance first realized that he was alive when he heard the unnatural wheeze beside him, as if Coalthorpe's entire body was now a faulty lung. In the center of his own abdomen was a gigantic void, but he choose not to look down. He rolled to his side, stared directly at the tousled hair atop Coalthorpe's bare head as it sifted gently to and fro in the breeze. His face was not visible. Spread behind him were small chunks of bright pink, glistening in the morning sunlight like delicate, fallen petals of wildflowers. Torrance blinked the objects into focus, identified them as pieces of Coalthorpe's lung.

Coalthorpe's voice was a whimper, and came after a long inward wheeze. "Mum...I take it...back..."

Torrance reached out and placed his fingertips in the shock of hair, waited the few seconds required for his friend's dying.

He rolled away from the body, pushed himself to a sitting position. The movement began what he knew would be another transformation, and the man looked down. To his surprise, there was no revulsion at the sight, only wonderment at how so much of his intestine hung from his belly. He reached down with his right hand and formed a protective cup around the gray mass, then looked back up the hill at the machine gun nest, saw dark eyes peering at him, saw the steam rising from the silent gun. It was then that Noel Torrance willed himself to gain his feet, careful to protect against spilling himself—a potential distraction he considered unacceptable in present circumstances—for he wished to leave the slayer of Devonshires with a riddle, and in the leaving, perhaps deny him pride. He fought against the swaying of his body, felt the pain begin to creep its way upward—a spreading fire—and then took the first step forward.

The eyes of every man in the machine-gun nest locked onto the lone British soldier. Werner Gruber slowly rotated the gun on its pivot, shifting his bulk along with Maschinengewehr 08 until the sights lined up with the faltering man. But still he came. Ten paces, then ten more, and the crew stared in disbelief at the grim, clenched-jaw face, at the long strand of intestine swinging like a pendulum from his right hand.

Stefan Hinkel said, "Finish the poor bastard. He is the last! You have killed them all!"

Gruber remained motionless, his hands frozen on the gun handles. "He...he is trying to speak."

"I don't want to hear him, Gruber, just finish it!"

"No."

When he was twenty paces from the muzzle of the gun, the soldier halted. He extended his left hand toward the Germans, and then his forefinger jutted upward from his fist simultaneous with a grunted word in his foreign language, and he jabbed the finger into his chest. Then a second word, as two fingers, pointing to the Germans, sprang from his fist. The word sounds grew louder in steady cadence, and he again pointed the single finger at his chest, the two fingers at the Germans, then again and again and again, until finally both of his arms flopped forward, released the wad of intestines, which swung to his knees.

Hinkel reached down, grabbed his rifle. "Enough, damn it! Shoot him...or I will."

Gruber said, "If you do, I will break both of your arms."

Hinkel turned away, slammed the rifle into the side of the nest.

The British soldier opened his mouth, but only silence hung in the air. He raised his head toward the crucifix, and then stretched his arms toward it, turned his palms upward, beseechingly. Only Gruber looked at him now, positioned him in the manner of a photographer, the tall rectangle of gun sight serving as frame. The soldier cried out a final time, but it was not a word, and then he disappeared from the frame.

Gruber pushed away from the gun, wearily gathered his weight over his haunches, and stood, stared at the body of the fallen soldier. Except for Hinkel, the other crew members lingered near the perimeter of the nest.

Hinkel said, "You waste your time pondering that last one, master gunner. Just one more filthy tribesmen...like all of us...and your god no more alive than this stone cross...or him."

"You are the fool, Stefan. How can you watch the courage of such a man...and yet believe he has no soul."

"He was insane...his guts in his hand...in agony. Like a wounded animal in its death throes!"

"His actions were...meaningful...somehow. He was not insane."

"Ahhh...'meaningful' you say, with his wild, counting fingers...one finger...two fingers...and chest pounding and pointing. And what did he mean...tell me!"

Gruber finally turned around, his face coated nearly black, cut with rivulets of sweat, his eyes beams of energy. "I do not know, but two things I do know: he was not insane… and the crucifix was far more than stone to him."

Hinkel clenched his teeth, fought off the impulse to spit out his final words on the matter. Instead, speaking evenly, calmly, he said, "You are a pair, master gunner…you and Maschinengewehr 08…the most efficient tribesman of all… and his spear. And one day, perhaps soon—a shell or a bomb-thrower slipping through—you will both be equal…in the dirt."

Gruber turned away, allowed the broken bits of friend-ship, or camaraderie, or whatever it had been, to spill from his soul. He said to the three crewmen, "Prepare to move."

At first, the men did not move, then, without resolve, began to shuffle about, and Gruber sensed their unease, read their minds.

"It does not matter that we have no orders. I will shoot no more from this place. Forever."

Stefan Hinkel never returned to his Black Forest home-land, nor did Werner Gruber ever solve the riddle. One hundred and thirteen days later, in the frozen midday of 21 October, the British eighteen-pounder shell found them in Regina Trench, only eight kilometers north of the crucifix. The trench became Hinkel's grave, with not a single trace of his broken body ever recovered.

Gruber lived in a netherworld for seventeen more days, finally succumbing in a military hospital at Beelitz, in Silesia. Members of the medical staff who closely attended him would, for many years to come, tell stories to their children— or anyone who would listen—about the ranting, maimed giant who clung tenaciously to life, apparently sustained by his quest to count beyond the number "two," a goal he never attained.

When Gruber's sheet-covered body was carried away, it passed under the dark, brooding eyes of a young, recovering soldier named Adolf Hitler, who watched in silence with his back pressed against a corridor wall, his head positioned directly under a small crucifix.

These scenes are taken from a published novel that I wrote, *Chambers*, and, with some alterations, serve to depict what is perhaps the nadir of human activity. I believe in Hell as surely as I believe in Heaven.

MARS

It was after one o'clock in the morning, but the bedroom light from Unit 2-B of The Cascades Apartments in southwest St. Louis glowed into the row of cedars that lined the rear boundary of the complex. Joey Fazor was working late. He was propped comfortably on two pillows pinched against the headboard of his bed. He had just showered, and had stood in cold water for a full minute in order to clear his head before he made his final selection. The sensual feel of the silk bathrobe was delightful, and he allowed himself a few more moments to concentrate on its caress.

Three eight-by-ten photographs of excellent quality lay on the sheet. He picked up the first and studied it carefully, as if for the first time, although essentially he had the boy's exquisite features memorized. He ticked off the pros and cons. Kansas City—great logistics regarding both pick-up from the snatch and delivery to the customer; solid two-man team with a good track record; very strong plusses, he nodded to himself. On the down side, his contact had stretched the truth about patterning the child's movements. Joey always knew when someone was lying to him—even the tiniest lie;

tiny lies could prove very costly in his line of work. Beyond this, the boy had not been seen without both parents alongside. He tossed the photograph back on the bed.

He picked up another one. Memphis—very suitable logistics; a man and a woman team with no history of screwups; again, a boy with excellent quality facial features and body. But the boy appeared to Joey to be an old nine, maybe ten, and he was big for his age, athletic looking, maybe a soccer type. A tough snatch for some pros, and he had used this team only once before. The photograph fell lightly on the first.

Joey picked up the last. Charlotte—the least desirable logistics of the three, but this was the only con. There was no doubt that this boy would make Mr. Kassley very happy. He looked at the smiling face in the photo. Somehow, Leva always managed to take the best shots. Leva and her gorilla brother were simply the best out there, no question. And they had him and his single mom patterned. Joey had known this was the boy even before the shower, but he had enjoyed the final selection process nonetheless; it had become a pleasing ritual.

He glanced at the radio clock; 2:10 Eastern Standard, but he would call anyway. Leva would want to know of his decision immediately. Besides, he smiled to himself, maybe she would be easier to deal with when she was a little sleep-fuzzy. He grabbed a pair of jeans and a tee shirt from the back of a chair and quickly dressed for the short ride to the phone booth.

The telephone on Leva Arstead's nightstand jangled three times before she answered thickly. "Who the hell is this?"

"Evenin', babe. I know it's late, but this car you're trying to sell me is really on my mind."

"Where you at?" The voice had lost its thickness.

"Three."

"Ten minutes."

Click.

Eight minutes later, Joey plucked the phone from its cradle. "Hello again, babe."

"I'm not in a chatty mood."

She did not hear his sigh of resignation. "It's a go with your kid. I'm not gonna waste our time trying to hassle over money with you. Top dollar. He's worth fifteen, and I know it, and I know you know it too, so…"

"Wait…wait, Joey. Where is it written down that's top dollar?"

"Come on, babe…"

"Don't fuck with me. I've heard through the vine that deals are going down way over twenty in Atlanta and Miami."

"Hey, Leva, this is the corn belt here where I am, and you ain't exactly in Miami yourself."

"I'm not saying he's worth that, Joey, but he's worth every penny of eighteen, and you damn well know it. Look, I'm not trying to keep you from making a decent living. But I know you got some high-roller chickenhawk on the hook, who's whackin' off over pictures, and now he's ready for the real deal. And I know that there's still a lot of room for your cut at eighteen. Me and Percy are down here looking at a mall snatch—rest room maybe…parking lot maybe—both tough snatches. And don't ever forget whose necks are on the block here, okay?"

"Hey…hey, I hear you, all right? Let me think on it till morn…"

"Here's the deal, Joey. I'm wide awake now and I'm not goin' back to bed before I make some other calls. You're not the only good mover out there. So, before you're all nice and comfy and tucked back in bed, this kid might be promised somewhere else, and it doesn't make a damn to me who I..."

"Easy...easy. I give up. We deal at eighteen."

Leva drew a long breath that Joey could not hear. "Good. We're set to try this Friday night. Have your guy on call. If we pull it off, we'll pass him to you in Nashville. Keep your phone handy between nine and ten your time."

Percy Arstead peered intently at his sister's deft fingers as they wielded the needle and thread. A long-sleeved gray work shirt was spread over her lap as she sewed the bright red logo of Southland Mall over the left breast pocket. Percy looked up at the lightweight nylon jacket hanging from the corner of a chair. He would wear it into the mall, and then, at the proper time, fold it and put it into his right rear trouser pocket. Percy could remove and fold the jacket into a neat square in precisely eight seconds. His left rear trouser pocket already bulged slightly with the two contractor-grade, black plastic trash bags. Percy had just finished lining one bag with the other and carefully refolding them into a precise square. At double strength, they could be trusted to contain up to eighty pounds without tearing. Percy had practiced, running in place for five minutes with eighty pounds, switching hands at thirty-second intervals. Such exercise was routine. Besides, by Leva's estimate, there would be a safety margin of eighteen pounds. His sister was incredibly accurate at estimating the weight of a child.

Percy reached up and adjusted the black-framed glasses with clear plastic lenses. He had worn them since noon, allowing himself ample time to become accustomed to their feel. The elastic headband that secured them was comfortably snug. Black athletic shoes were light and perfect on his feet, with the strings double-knotted and well above floor level.

Percy returned his focus to his sister, whose gaze had not moved from her lap for the last five minutes. He stole a glimpse at her face and reflected on the undeniable fact, as he had a hundred times before, that she looked like their father, although the man's memory was a blank slate in his brain. It was impossible for him to imagine that his mother's eyes could have been such cold steel, and the mirror reveled to Percy that his eyes were very different from Leva's.

He looked quickly back at her hands; it was never a good idea to look at Leva's face for very long. It was as if she could see into his brain and sort out the electrical impulses that gave life to his thoughts. And if she saw him peeking at her now, she would know that he was thinking soft thoughts— thoughts of long-dead parents, thoughts that could interfere with the life that Leva had structured for him now. She had structured things for him as long as he could remember. They were united as one; it had always been so. His memory had shut out many things long past, things of dread and night- mares. But he could still remember some of the night sounds that came from Arthur Finley's bedroom on the top floor of the three-story children's home tucked away in the tall pines of southern Georgia, and he could remember his sister's face as the pale light of morning unmasked her grim features, and he knew that the sounds and the grimness were linked. And he could remember the night that they had walked away from the place, never to look back.

He had asked her once, when he was eleven and she was thirteen, about their parents. The look of her eyes in that instant was seared for all time in his brain, and he saw a malignancy that sucked the breath from him. Seventeen years had passed, and he had never again mentioned their parents.

She was finished, and held up the shirt to inspect her handiwork. Satisfied, she turned to Percy and handed it to him, made him look into her eyes for a moment. "It's time to go." She cocked her head and raised her eyebrows, smiled coldly. "World isn't gonna run out of kids, and we're not gonna run out of money."

The woman seated beside the younger man at a table in Café Court sipped her Coke through a long straw, filling her mouth with the sweet liquid and holding it there for delicious moments before swallowing. Her hair, drawn into a tight bun on top of her head, held a faintly grayish tint that was not there the day before. Her visage was wan, totally devoid of makeup, and her blouse was plain and dull white, tucked into faded blue jeans. Leva Arstead appeared as a harmless, nondescript woman of fifty.

Percy sipped ice water directly from his tall paper cup; he preferred to work without a trace of caffeine in his bloodstream. His performance would span only a few minutes, and if it was precise and machine-like, Leva would be very happy, as would Joey Fazor. And when Joey was made happy, a double-lined grocery sack full of small bills would be theirs. The consequence of slightly sloppy work would be the loss of the sack and Leva's displeasure—not small things—but the consequence of very sloppy work might well be a prison term. Percy did not dwell on such possibilities. His body was a wondrous mechanism, and within it he could release the perfect amount of adrenaline—a great rush or a small spurt—to tackle the work at hand. Leva's short fingernails tapped insistently on the table, and he looked with her at perhaps three dozen exiting moviegoers shuffling from the theater area into Café Court. He spotted the mother and son as they walked in front of the food vendors and on toward the arcade.

"Hope he had lots of soda in the movie," Percy said.

He could see Leva's head nodding before she spoke. "Did last Friday."

Percy moved his head a quarter turn to face the wall and picked out a light fixture as a focal point. He stared at it until it became a fuzzy, faraway object, and only then did he mentally rehearse what he was about to do.

It would not matter if the boy chose the child-level urinal or a stall. The boy would pay no attention to the janitor with the plastic trash bag until he had zipped up his trousers and turned around. The janitor would be on his right knee, and his eyes would be on the same level as the boy's, and when the child froze in that instant of inquiry—in that perfect half second—it would happen. The jab would be thrown with the speed of a snake's tongue from no more than fifteen inches, directly onto the point of the chin. It would be forceful enough to crush an orange without exposing the pulp. The small body would never touch the floor; it would be gathered quickly into the double trash bag, and the janitor would be free to leave.

The tap of Leva's finger came to his arm, not the table. "What are you doing?"

"Just thinking the deal over, Sis...just practicing in my head."

She paused and cocked her head. "You okay, Percy?"

"Sure, never better. No problem."

"That's good."

They both turned their attention back to the arcade entry. The minutes ticked by; the crowd was thinning out nicely. It was almost time to go to work.

The boy jammed a small fist into the air as the last of the space invaders fell to the might of his ray gun. "Did you see that, Mom? Never had a chance, did he?"

"You are definitely the baddest invader zapper in Charlotte." She tousled his hair.

"Mom, I gotta go pee, and then…"

"No 'and then', buddy. Poor old Mom wants to curl up at home with a little T.V. before bedtime."

"But I still do gotta pee."

"I can wait for that. Let's go."

Fifty feet away, the apron-clad attendant cleared the two tall paper cups from the empty table.

The mother watched intently as her son entered the men's room, and then took her place across the narrow corridor. She paid little attention to the woman who stood facing away from her, six steps down the corridor, near the door to the women's room.

Inside the men's room, the boy glanced around and saw only the janitor preparing to change trash bags. He picked out the nearest stall and pushed the door open, latched it behind him.

The belly of the fat man spilled over his plaid trousers, leading the way down the corridor like the rounded prow of a small ship bobbing through choppy water. Leva had locked her peripheral vision on the man from the time he turned off of the main mall walkway. He was wearing a watch; Leva knew that all would be well. Ten more huffing steps, and then she would step in front of him, humbly begging his pardon, and inquire of the time. She would then ask him if he was sure about the accuracy of his timepiece, quietly incredulous as to the lateness of the hour and the whereabouts of her elderly mother. Was there a security guard close by? Would he assist her in locating guard? The delay would last as long as required.

He galumphed forward, was three steps away now, and as Leva took a steadying breath and gathered herself, she heard the faint squeak of the men's room door. The fat man barreled past her and nearly collided with the janitor as he slipped past the door, a full trash bag in his right hand.

"Hey, sorry, bub," the fat man laughed, "I'm about to bust."

The janitor did not look up or reply.

The mother barely glanced at the janitor with the bright logo on his work shirt and the full bag in his hand. The man moved unhurriedly down the corridor and she directed her gaze to the fat man, who was as harmless looking as any man could be. She did not notice that the woman in the corridor was gone.

The first sixty seconds passed easily enough, but with the passing of sixty more, the seed of apprehension took root. She chased the silly little thought away and shook her head at a mother's capacity for paranoia. Thirty more, and she could not chase it away. *Surely,* the fat man was nothing to worry... The door was opening. The fleshy round face contorted into a polite smile.

"Excuse me, sir, I hate to bother you, but my son seems to be taking a rather long time...and..."

It was when the man's eyes registered puzzlement at her statement that the woman felt the horror close around her throat like a pair of strong hands. She shoved him aside and jerked the door open, flashed through the opening. The first sound that came from the men's room seemed to the fat man like that of someone strangling, but it was the next sound that sent him careening down the corridor for help. It was the sound of a woman dying in agony.

The rear door of the van opened as Percy approached. He gently swung the plastic bag into the rear compartment as Leva guided it in. He moved quickly to the driver's seat and started the engine. He peeled off his shirt and tossed it back to Leva, who handed him a plain black tee shirt. Within seconds, the big vehicle accelerated smoothly and rolled out of the parking lot. Leva tore away the plastic bags, found the boy's left arm, and plunged the needle deep into the deltoid muscle. He groaned faintly and his head flopped toward her, but he did not open his eyes. She then stripped the child naked and made a careful inspection, using the beam of a small flashlight like a surgical tool as it swept from head to toe. The bruise on his chin was angry looking, but the jawbone and lower teeth were unharmed. His skin was flawless, the sturdy body well-proportioned. A chickenhawk's delight. Now that she had time to look closely, Leva was sorry that she had not fought for another thousand. Along with Percy's shirt, she wadded the child's clothing into a ball and tucked it into the remnants of the plastic bags, and later that night she would watch the ball burn. She dressed the child in new clothing—white underwear, dark sweat suit, white cotton socks, and black athletic shoes. She positioned the ice bag over his chin, propping it with a folded blanket, and then tucked more blankets along the sides of his body. She crawled into the front seat.

"Very nice work, Percy."

"Thanks. What was the deal with the fat guy at the door?"

"I was one second away from jumping him when I heard the door, but it worked out."

"Couldn't have gone better."

"First C-store past the edge of town, we'll stop and find a phone. I got a happy call to make to Mr. Joey Fazor."

They drove for three more blocks before the black and white police cruiser pulled alongside the van at a red light. Neither Percy nor Leva registered the slightest alarm; it had been a perfect snatch.

Leva said, "Ain't life strange, Percy? Mister Policeman has got a high-cap nine mil pistol on his belt, a twelve-gauge stoked with buckshot against the console, a radio that could call in a dozen more like him in two minutes, three-hundred fifty horses under the hood, and all that separates the hero from the kid is a little sheet metal and six feet of air." She made a sound in her chest—a purr of satisfaction. "The son-of-a-bitch might as well be on Mars."

Over a period of several years while traveling a familiar rural route, I have observed a lonely, raggedy donkey standing in a field. On more than one occasion thoughts of releasing it from the bonds of earth have crept into my mind. A year has passed since I last saw it, and when I drive by the empty field, my mind wanders into the strange realm wherein human foibles and imperfections ricochet off one another like a handful of lead pellets dropped on a hard surface.

THE GOD OF DONKEYS

All living creatures are a mystery, more so after they die.

The man turned west off of the highway and drove slowly over the frozen gravel road, looked to his left across the barbed wire fence and into the snow-patched field, a ragged checkerboard that stretched to the woods line. But the man saw neither the field nor the woods, his gaze fixed thirty steps distant on the little donkey with the stubbly wisp of a mane and a thin tail that shifted to and fro at the whim of the icy wind that knifed from the north across the road and into the field. The animal's gray-dun coat was scruffy and thin, his ribs furrowed beneath the hide like the form of a boat hull under construction, yet with a wormy pot-belly sagging below. He appeared to stare straight ahead, as if there were an object worthy of donkey contemplation somewhere in the empty bleakness of late February. The muzzle and eye rings, once white, were filthy and crusted, the long pointed ears jutting forward like worn horns. His hooves were hidden in the dead grass, but the man suspected that they were curled upward, unclipped, perhaps with abscesses.

The man braked the new, black 1978 Chevrolet pickup truck, jammed the gear selector up into park. He looked back to the front, stared for long moments through the windshield at the low iron clouds scudding from north to south. He counted backwards, a winter at a time, settled on three as the accurate number over which, every two or three weeks, he had seen the donkey in the field, never more than a few feet from where it stood now, rooted in the harsh earth as surely as an unwanted scrub cedar or Osage Orange. The man's job dictated his present travel route mostly in winter, but he was certain that the warmer months were only marginally better for the pathetic, unloved creature. The man swung open the door, climbed out, straightened his lanky frame. He was thirty-one years old, carried no excess flesh, and squinted out of long habit. On the back of his left hand was a black tattoo of excellent design that read: 101st AIRBORNE, and under that, the head of a screaming eagle. From the pocket of his denim work shirt he fingered a Marlboro cigarette, tucked it between his lips, and then lit it with a Zippo bearing the same design as the tattoo. He smoked half in four long draws and then tossed the long stub into the snow filled ditch. He turned back to the open cab, bent forward at the waist, and reached under the seat. He grasped the holstered revolver in his left hand, and with his right withdrew the six-inch-barreled Smith and Wesson Model 29, tossed the holster in the seat. The nickel plating gleamed even in the low light. The cylinder was loaded with six .44 magnum cartridges, hand loaded, each bullet two hundred forty grains in weight and in a jacketed hollow point configuration. The cases contained twenty-three grains of high quality smokeless powder. With a quarter turn of his head to his left, he paused, looked and listened for approaching vehicles. There was only the wind in his ears. He took a two-handed hold on the black rubber grips as he placed his forearms across the top of the door, and then cocked the hammer with his left thumb. The front sight with the red insert settled into the square notch of the rear sight. His eyes focused on the insert, the top of which was now aligned at a point two inches behind the left eye of the donkey. As it always was when targets lived and breathed, the report of the gun did not come to the man's ears as a loud noise; rather, a fading echo wafting across the barren landscape. The donkey disappeared from the sight picture, and the man knew that there was no need to look down. He turned quickly, slid the revolver back into the holster, shoved it back under the seat. He settled back into the seat and drove a few yards forward before making a three-point turn back toward the paved road.

Eight hundred yards to the south, and hidden atop a wooded ridge, a frame house squatted in a copse of elm trees. Ensconced within the living room, a couple sat in green vinyl lounge chairs as they stared at the fuzzy images cast from an eighteen-inch black and white television set, the rabbit ears above it sagging and wrapped with clumps of aluminum foil. The man's hair was still thick, though greying around the edges; incrementally, one year slipping into the next, he had come to care less and less about its length. His wife's hair, in short tight curls, was more grey than black, but this fact caused her no more care than did the thirty pounds that had crept onto her frame over the past twenty years. The man's thick forearms rested in his lap, and on the right forearm was a faded tattoo peeking through the hair that read: 101st AIRBORNE, and under that, the image of a screaming eagle.

In the kitchen, another man sat at the small oval table, his wide face expressionless, rivulets of saliva cutting crookedly from both corners of his mouth. His hair was buzz-cut on the sides to a line just above his ears, and above the line it was only twice as long. He was twenty seven years old, did not tolerate the smelly fuel-oil heat in the living room any better than he tolerated people, including his parents. In wintertime he spent most of his hours in the drafty kitchen shirtless and barefoot, as he was now. The man was vaguely aware that the seasons of the year bore names, but he sensed with great clarity the fact that soon the last of the snow would melt, the sun would rise higher and warmer, and that he again would lead his donkey to the shade of the trees and wait with his silent friend until the breeze found them, and then he would feed him carrots from his hand. And the man knew that even today, in the cold and before darkness, he would make his daily trek down to the low field and lead his donkey back up the hill and into the shelter. Robot-like, he poked a kernel of corn through the wires of a bird cage sitting in the middle of the table. The cage contained a young fox squirrel that chattered as it approached the kernel. Two huge cats, a yellow and a grey, both with long fur, slinked with arched backs and stilted legs back and forth between his bare ankles. On the linoleum floor beside his chair, a tan colored mongrel lay curled, its dark eyes peering upward and locked on the noisy squirrel.

In the living room, the woman asked the man, "You hear that?"

"I did in fact."

"Gun?"

"Yes 'twas, but not a shotgun."

"On us?"

"Yes 'twas."

"What you reckon?"

"Somebody takin' a whack at a runnin' coyote comes to mind. They will make a trot through sometimes in the middle of the day...or dig for mice in the snow."

The man steered the Chevy pickup onto the paved road, but for only a hundred feet before he glanced into the rearview mirror, slammed the brakes and shifted into reverse. The tires squealed faintly to a halt at the intersection with the gravel road and then he turned back onto it, rolling slowly, past the still form of the donkey's body, and on for a quarter mile until he stopped at a mailbox. It was fashioned from an old black metal lunch pail, and mounted on top of a cedar fence post leaning westward. Painted white in sturdy block lettering was a single name: G I S H. The man looked south down the narrow lane—a packed bed of two-inch rock, thin but serviceable—and followed its trace across the end of the field and up the long rise where it disappeared into the trees. He turned the truck down the lane and drove slowly as he lit a cigarette. The north wind caught the little cloud of smoke slipping from the driver's-side window and chased it ahead of the truck until it vanished.

He peered through the windshield as the truck topped the rise, and he spied the house, a far better vision than the one that had begun to form in his mind as he drove up the lane. It was old, to be sure, but the asbestos-clad walls were square, the asphalt-shingled roof sound and properly guttered, the window frames a reasonable shade of white. A small wooden porch, roofed and shingled, harbored a green front door with a brass knocker. The man braked to a halt, ground the cigarette stub in the console ashtray. Stacked one on top of the other at the corner of the porch sat two small, empty animal cages with trap doors for live catching. Behind the house was a metal shed that appeared even sturdier than the house, and from behind the shed the front half of a weathered, yellow bulldozer intruded into the grey light, its tall blade aligned with a goose-necked trailer. The front yard was no more than a forty foot square, uncluttered with items either abandoned or neglected that the man had been certain he would see. A bird feeder was centered in one half of the yard, which was divided by a concrete walk, and centered in the other half was a twenty-foot flagpole with a three-foot by four-foot American flag rippling in the breeze.

The dog in the kitchen low-growled the presence of the truck in the driveway, but his master rubbed the toes of his right foot against the dog's ribs, silencing it, and then he looked into the living room as he heard the engine stop. He watched his mother push herself up from her chair and shuffle toward the door. The man let the corn kernels slip from his hand onto the table as he pushed the chair back and stood. He slipped to the open doorway to the living room, and then hid behind the wall.

She did not wait for the knock on the door before opening it a foot and poking out her head. The approaching man had a chiseled, handsome face and was wearing an unzipped camouflage hunting jacket. He stopped six paces from the porch. "Is this the Gish residence?"

She nodded, said, "Don't believe we've met."

"Do you own the field with the donkey?"

She nodded again, furrowed her brow. "What's that to you?"

The man shifted his weight, reset his boots in the grass, stuffed his hands into his coat pockets. "Is Mister Gish around?"

Her eyes did not move from the man. She was certain now, the dread rising in the space between them like a stench. "Vinis Gish, come forth!"

The door opened wide, the frame filled with the bulk of Vinis Gish, his broad, square hands thumb-hooked over the suspenders of his bib overalls. For several seconds, the two men studied each other's faces, probing, seeking clues. Gish said, "What's this here about?"

The man drew in a steady breath, released it slowly. "For years I've passed by that little donkey down in your field and wondered when somebody would ever take proper care of it." He paused, studied Gish's eyes for a reaction, saw a gear shift in the man's head as surely as if metal teeth were meshing.

"The gun shot was your'n?"

"It was."

The woman's voice, low and plaintive, wafted past her husband's shoulder. "Holy Jeeeeesus ...Lil' Clem."

Gish said, "We have a terrible situation here."

"I could've just drove on away...started to, but it wouldn't have been right. I'm not that kind of man."

"So you come up here to tell me what kind of a sorry-ass man I am, that it?"

"No. I came so you'd know that it wasn't a vandal with no reason."

"Donkey just as dead though, ain't he?" Gish lowered his hands to his hips. "Who made you god of donkeys?"

The man's hands slipped from his pockets. "Look, Gish...I didn't come here to start a fight over this. I came as a point of honor, and if it helps, I'd be willing to pay you for your trouble if you want to dispose of the carcass."

"You got any kids?"

"Yes...boy and a girl."

"They normal?"

The man's brow crinkled. "Normal?"

"Of the mind, I mean."

51

The man swallowed, nodded, said nothing.

"That is a blessing you'll never really understand, mister god of donkeys."

Gish's eyes reddened as he stepped forward from the door and walked across the porch into the grass. He stopped three feet from the man. "Let me tell what you've done... and how much your goddamned honor's worth." He raised a fist and motioned over his shoulder toward the door. "In there is our boy who was born slow of the mind. He understands most everything, but he don't...or can't...no damn doctor knows for sure...say a word, never has. Sorta like the talkin' world is a mystery he don't care to participate in... which may make him smarter than all us talkers. He will live with us like a man-child till we're dead and then the state will have to keep him until he's dead. And the only things in this entire world he cares about are his animals...and that little donkey which woulda likely lived another twenty years... well, I reckon he loved that critter most of all. Speakin' of which, I just spent sixteen dollars and thirty-four cents on wormin' medicine which the vet claimed was gonna finally fix him. And further speakin' of which, a farrier that knows him by name comes regular and tends his hooves. And further speakin' of which, had a shelter just in the trees yonder which he could get in when he wanted...which wasn't often, I know not why...because most donkeys would...but not Lil' Clem."

Gish stopped for breath and knuckled a tear into his cheek, clenched his jaws. He lowered his head, and the man in front of him took it as a sign of gathering calm, and he too lowered his head. It was then when the blow loosed an explosion behind his left eye, and when he looked up the tree tops moved in sweeping circles, as if a summer wind storm had invaded his head. Time slowed, trickling now, the tree tops slowing too, and finally the man raised his hand, fingered the blood leaking from his the corner of his eye. He propped himself on one elbow, allowed the details of the preceding minutes to re-form in the returning chambers of his brain. He glanced up, saw that Gish had not moved, and then steadied himself on one knee before regaining his feet. From his hip pocket he pulled a red handkerchief and held it against his mouth for several seconds. The only sounds in the yard were the frettings of a brace of crows, high overhead and discordant with the soft whoosh of the wind. Gish raised his right hand, no longer a fist.

"You take your honorable self away from here and don't come back...ever."

"Reckon I had that comin'. I am sorry for all the trouble."

As the man turned toward his truck, a flicker of movement to his right and at the corner of the house invaded Gish's peripheral vision. He turned his head and saw the barrel of the shotgun, but before he could open his mouth to shout, the roar echoed past him, and when he jerked his head back to the front the man was coiled in agony, his boots churning in the colorless grass. As Gish ran to the stricken man, he heard his wife scream behind him. The man rolled onto his back, then struggled to a sitting position. He spread his jacket and ripped open his shirt, three white buttons popping into the air. He made no sound as he stared down at the seeping exit holes that formed a ragged pattern spread over six inches of his abdomen. Gish dropped to his knees, placed his left hand behind the man's head and carefully lowered him to the ground. He reached down with his right hand and found the bloody left hand and he squeezed it with a gentle pressure. From inside the house, the dog barked inquisitively and without pause, seeking his master's whereabouts.

Gish looked at the holes that he knew to be the result of a double ought buckshot load from a twelve gauge shell, and with the knowledge he knew that the man was doomed. "Goddammit all! Goddammit, man!" He shook his shaggy head from side to side.

The man's words wheezed upward, fading sounds, but Gish heard them. "Am I dead?"

Gish nodded, said, "Yes."

"Thought that." His eyelids sank halfway, then his eyeballs fixated in death.

Gish held onto the limp hand for a moment, then looked down as it slid free, the tattoo now in full view. The black numerals and letters and the image of the screaming eagle of the 101st Airborne burned a hole that reached into the middle of Gish's head, then down to his gut, and he gagged, swallowed against the nausea pooled at the base of his tongue. He planted one foot underneath his body, then the other, and pushed himself upright. He felt his wife's shoulder crowd against his, but he separated from her touch, could not deal with the trembling. From inside the house, the dog barking suddenly ceased.

The woman's voice was a loud whisper. "Lord God, Vinis…what we gonna do?"

Gish pressed his fingertips against his forehead, and then lowered his hands to his waist, locked his fingers. "Be still a minute, woman…got to think here."

She waited as long as she could stand the silence, a span of sixty seconds that she was certain had covered several minutes. "They'll carry him away, won't they?… pen him up somewhere where he can't have his animals…Lord God…"

"No…ain't nobody gonna carry him away." He unlocked his fingers, raised his head, straightened his arms, then spoke in an even tone, like a man talking into a mirror, delivering a statement of great import to himself. "The only one that acted outside his bounds here was a man that shoulda' known better." He shook his head, slowly, steadily. "Our family will not pay for his mistake…in any manner." Gish looked straight up into the low clouds for a moment, then back level, considered it appropriate to the occasion that the sun was not visible. "I will take down our flag to tie around him and then we will load him into his truck and I will drive it down behind this hill to the open glade where the rock won't be shelved in the ground. I will take the tractor and go drag Lil' Clem to the same place. Then I'll fire up the dozer and go down there and dig a hole ten feet deep and thirty feet wide. Into that hole I will put and mash down to near nothin' the truck, which will be the man's casket, and I will put Lil' Clem beside it, and then I will fill the hole and brush it over and make it look like it has been that way for a long time. All the while, you will tend the boy inside the house and be sure his mind is on his critters. It will be over before night-fall. It will be days, more likely weeks, before any laws might poke around after a missing man who traveled the blacktop road. They might never come. But if they do, I will be the one to talk."

He turned to his wife, made her red-rimmed, weepy eyes hold his until he was certain that she wouldn't look away. He said, "Can you live with that arrangement, woman…now and forever?"

Her chin quivered, her hands a white knot of bone, thinly covered with flesh. "I'll have to." She swallowed thickly, sucked in a quick breath. "I saw his tattoo, Vinis. Can you?"

Great tears rolled down his cheeks, and he stifled a sob that racked his barrel chest. He steadied himself, said. "In time….I'll have to."

At a quarter past four o-clock in the afternoon, on a Saturday that marked the end of the second week of March, a Moniteau County Sheriff's patrol car rolled slowly to a halt in front of the Gish house. When the deputy stepped from his vehicle, he looked down the path toward the metal shed and watched as Vinis Gish ambled toward him. When he was twenty feet from the deputy, Gish hailed the younger man with a toss of his right hand and said, "Howdy there, young fella, what can I do for ya?"

"Well, sir...Mr. Gish, I take it?" Gish nodded in affirmation. "I'm helping with a search effort regarding a missing person that you might've heard about."

Gish nodded. "Seems like I heard somethin' about it on the news a couple weeks ago maybe. Somebody from down around Springfield, they say?"

"Yes, a man named Worth Strother, thirty-one, dark hair, six-two, around two hundred pounds...most likely wearing a camo jacket. Last seen in a new black Chevy pickup. He travelled regular between Columbia and Springfield, most often over on Highway 63 down through Lake Ozarks, but his wife said he liked to get off the beaten path every so often." The deputy flapped his hands as if in apology. "The Highway Patrol, County Sheriffs all around, City Police...you name it...we've been near about everywhere by now I reckon. But you never know when you might run into somebody who saw something, heard something." He flapped his hands again, and then reset his Smokey Bear hat. "Anyway...we're pretty much stumped by it all...heckuva mystery, I'll say. Sorry for the bother."

"No bother a'tal."

The deputy swung the car door open, swept his gaze back over the house and the surrounding trees. "Nice place you got here. Quiet and private, up on this hill. Like to have a place like this myself someday. He paused, flipped a hand. "Oh…and for what it's worth, he had a tattoo on the back of his left hand. 101st Airborne thing, had the screaming eagle head under it."

What Vinis Gish then did was something that he would never fully comprehend; he would only remember that he had no control over the rising of his right arm, or over his left hand as it unbuttoned the shirt sleeve and peeled it back to his elbow, or over his voice. "Like this most likely."

The deputy squinted and then stepped towards Gish, looked closely. "Well, I'll be danged…you too, huh?"

"World War Two. Place called Bastogne is what we're remembered for most, I reckon."

The deputy took off his hat, extended his hand. "Well, I'll be…you were one of the Battered Bastards of Bastogne?"

Gish shook his hand, said, "Still am."

"This is an honor, Mr. Gish…to be sure."

"Oh, I 'spect not as much as you think. We were just scared boys…tryin' to make it to the next day…same thing everybody tries to do in this life."

"Well, you'd be interested to know that Strother took a Silver Star in Vietnam…place called A…something…valley, I think."

"A Shau Valley…that would be the place." Gish paused, closed his eyes for a second. "This makes him a double sad story for me."

The deputy looked up at the flag, said, "I'm sure it does. I might've known you were a vet. Not many folks fly flags that nice. Looks near new."

Gish nodded, looked up at it with the deputy. "It is. I put a new one up every spring…retired the old one a little early this year."

86327314

"Well, I better get on my way. Couple more stops before I get off."

"So long, son."

Gish watched as the deputy backed the patrol car away from the yard, braked, and then began to drive forward down the lane. Gish raised his right arm in a final farewell.

The wind calmed as the cold of twilight seeped up the hill and found Vinis Gish, who sat on the edge of the front porch. He wore his Army fatigue jacket over his coveralls, and on his feet were worn but sturdy combat boots. His head cover was his Army overseas cap, now a half size too small because he no longer took regular haircuts. Leaning on the porch beside him was a wooden-handled garden spade. In the right pocket of his jacket was a ring box that had not held a ring for over thirty years. After a time, Gish stood, waited for the stiffness to smooth out, and then began to walk south. He passed the shed and proceeded down a path that was roughly defined in grass still dead to the cling of winter. He thought ahead, two months into spring, to the time when he would walk in the bright of day, swing his Kaiser blade through green grass and more precisely define the path.

The moon a was halved orb, clean and gleaming, casting freely its white light, the precise shade of which Gish had never seen replicated by the hand of man anywhere on the earth that he had trod for fifty-six years. He stopped at the edge of the glade, waited for the light to settle on the quarter-ton Chert boulder that he had bladed into place over the bodies of Worth Strother and Lil' Clem. He walked to the boulder and sat down on it, propped the spade against the stone. He leaned back, braced his upper body with his arms, felt the gritty cold of the Chert under his palms and fingers. Since the day of the burial, Vinis Gish had accomplished more hours of contemplation on realms both high and low than he had in the aggregate of his life before that day. The fact that he had already lived the majority of his days no longer pricked at him with a single, clawed finger as it once did. The reality of death within a rapidly decreasing span of years was nearly, but not quite yet, a comfort. What had been foreboding doom—seldom thought of and quickly chased away when it did slip past his guard—had been transformed into what he hoped was a spiritual foretaste of the higher realm. But it was only a hope, wispy and ephemeral, for no man could be certain of such things. And so it was that now he contemplated the layers of iron and organic matter—fragments of the low realm of earth—that had been compressed over eons unfathomable into the Chert marker. Beneath the boulder, the bodies of both man and animal had begun the process that would in mere decades—eye blinks in eternity— compress their matter, return the cells of flesh and bone to the earth from whence they came. Airy hope on high, stony reality down low; Vinis Gish was certain that he would be tugged back and forth between the two realms until they were sorted out and made clear to him in a place beyond Death, or until Death reigned in a vast black void.

He rocked his weight forward, stood, picked up the spade. At the base of the boulder he dug a hole, a foot wide and four feet deep. He stabbed the spade into the ground and reached into his jacket pocket, pulled out the box, opened it. He looped the ball chain over the tip of his right finger and lifted it until his dog tags rose to eye level, where they rotated in the moonlight for several seconds before he released them back into the box and replaced the lid. He knelt and reached into the hole as far as he could, then opened his fingers, freed the box. With the point of the spade, Gish drug chunks of soil and small stones into the hole, pausing every half foot to tamp the fill solid. He rested the handle of the spade across his right shoulder and began to retrace his path through the grass and up the hill. On a bluff top a half mile distant, coyotes began to howl and yip, and the man stood still, listened until the last of the haunting notes faded away, and then he wondered for a time if the sounds were heard in the high realm or if they died in the tree tops of the low realm. He looked up the hill before him, saw the yellow rectangles of light from the house, and then he began to walk toward them.

The man wearing a bright red St. Louis Cardinals baseball cap watched from the edge of the glade as the operator of the yellow Caterpillar high-lift maneuvered expertly, the great bucket gouging and digging into the pliable ground. The man stood with his left hand resting on the top of a two-by-four driven into the ground, and stapled to the board was a building permit issued by The County of Moniteau, Missouri, dated: April 10, 2008. A Chert boulder lay in temporary repose on the low side of the glade, having been shoved there by the high-lift operator, who knew that the landowner would covet the stone as a jewel for the landscaping that would adorn the yard of the splendid, brick home that would soon rise from the ground, as now were the awakening blossoms of purple Henbit and white clover, and the Honeysuckle, its inimitable perfume delicate on the breeze. The big engine throttled low, then into idle, and finally chugged to a halt. The operator climbed down from the cab, and when his boots hit the ground he hailed the man in the cap with the sweep of his arm.

The operator—sixtyish, wiry, and clad in a blaze orange hunting jacket—waited until the man stood beside him in front of the toothed-bucket. They looked down at the mud-caked clump of twisted metal that was only slightly larger than a refrigerator box. The operator tilted back his head and took a long swig from a plastic bottle of Mountain Spring water, then asked, "Know what that is?"

The man studied the unnatural object for a few seconds. "Shit...looks like a vehicle...or parts of one."

"That it would be."

"Why here I wonder?"

"Not many rocks. Same reason your house is going here. Must've come from the old Gish place that was up there on the hill. Old Vinis ran a dozer in those days...my dad knew him some, but nobody ever knew him too well." He took another swig of water. "You'd be surprised how many old cars I've dug up over the years. House foundations, pasture terraces, digging ponds...lakes. I drained an old pond once, and not a big one, that had five of these in the bottom." He paused, peered at the newfound problem. "Never saw one crunched down like that though."

"Humm...well, I suppose that it's an issue, you know, with..."

"Yeah, I know where you're going, and the answer is maybe."

"I'm listening."

"If we go by DNR regs, things get way more complicated... and expensive...than they ought to be."

"And if we don't?"

"If that was to take place, it would mean that just you, me, the crows and squirrels and some coyote that's likely watching us from somewhere, and the like, will be the only ones who know that the new burial ground will be over there at the base of the berm to your new fish pond...which I can go commence right now…and then come back here and finish with your foundation hole."

"I can keep a secret with all those things."

"Figured that."

"Story goes that nobody ever figured out how the house burned with them all in it."

"My dad says there was a hassle between Gish's brother and the insurance company about how the fire got started. Don't know how that turned out…been what, fifteen years now?"

"That sounds about right."

"Well, anyhow, Dad claims that their boy…bad retarded, living with 'em…was in the middle of it all. Nuttier'n a damn fruitcake towards the end. Dad says he took to standing out in that field that borders the road…rain, cold…didn't matter…they couldn't do thing with him. Dad saw him a couple times. Damndest deal."

"Man, that's sad."

"Sure as hell is."

The operator turned and climbed back into his seat, fired the engine and edged forward. The teeth of the bucket slid easily underneath the burden. With a hydraulic whine, the bucket rose from the ground and the machine clanked away. The man walked forward and idly toed his boot over the damp soil, and on a hand-sized clump of mud he spied a patch of material in a faded pattern. He bent down, peeled the patch from the clump. He placed it in the palm of his hand, smoothed it with a fingertip. There was no doubt that once it had been part of a camouflage garment, obviously a part of something totally worn out even before it had been left in the vehicle. Or, he thought, it could have been a blunder of forgetfulness, or maybe it had belonged to Gish's crazy son, meaning that it wasn't a blunder at all, but just the odd way of some things. He turned his hand over, released the patch. "Oh well…dust to dust," he said aloud.

From the edge of the woods, two piercing caw caws hung in the air, then faded away, and the man reckoned that a crow had affirmed his benediction, and that the creature was as qualified to do so as most of the people he knew, or had ever known.

When I was fifteen, we had a lean-on-the-fence-and-gab neighbor named Frank who was a prison guard at the Missouri State Penitentiary, in Jefferson City, Missouri, located twenty-two miles from our little hometown of California. In the early 1960's, this institution was widely regarded as one of the most hardcore state prisons in the nation. On occasion, Frank related scenes that he had witnessed inside the belly of the beast that my father had no desire to hear. I don't remember exactly what I might have said (if indeed anything at all) that triggered what Pop said to me late one afternoon after a session with Frank, but I will never forget what he said: "Son, I could deal with your death easier than I could with you being down there in the pen." No more was ever said between us about his pronouncement. No more was required. A son and grandsons later, Edwin Denbow came to life.

ABSOLUTIONS

The Sorting of Edwin Denbow

The body of the 1952 Chevrolet pickup was colorless, save for random, faint blue swaths that had survived thirteen years of hard life. Avery Kettle drew deeply on his Camel, touched the tip of his tongue to a fragment of tobacco on his lower lip and shot it forward with a long jet of smoke. It was his fourth cigarette, three chain lit. He was shirtless under ragged, denim bib overalls, the sweat-stained straps draped over massive, hairy shoulders. Atop his head was a serviceable straw hat, canted toward the late afternoon August sun, and worn but sturdy brogans protected his feet. Kettle considered a man's head and feet to be generally the only body parts to be coddled. He shuffled the toe of a brogan in the gravel at the edge of Paddy Creek Road, two miles north of Highway 50 and eighteen miles west of Jefferson City, Missouri, and the great pen of men surrounded by the high stone walls that had once been his home for four thousand and eighty-one days. He took another drag and the smoke streamed in an arc as his head swiveled left down the road toward the dust cloud of an approaching vehicle. As it drew near, Kettle made it out to be a white Ford Falcon, a '61 or '62, he reckoned.

The driver cut the engine, but did not move from behind the wheel, his fingers locked around the top, as if the machine still needed guidance. Kettle watched as the man's head tilted back with the effort to fill his lungs. Slowly, the door creaked partially open, but only for a moment, and then it latched back with a thud. The driver lifted his fingers, looked at Kettle, waited.

Kettle pinched the Camel stub between his thumb and forefinger, sucked out the last drag and flicked it away as he approached the open window.

The man said, "I'd rather talk in the car."

Kettle walked to the passenger side, got in and rolled the window down. He looked the man over: late forties, slight build, balding, glasses in a heavy black frame, unremarkable features—a very plain man. Kettle had followed the story in the papers, but mainly on the grapevine, and thought he remembered that Edwin Denbow worked for Sears and

Roebuck, or some such, down in Jeff City. The phone call had come late the previous night.

Kettle said, "Still curious about how you found me. You were cloudy on that."

"Not many ex-cons in Moniteau County. Word gets around."

Kettle made a sound in his chest, nodded his head. "You said twenty bucks on the phone."

Denbow fingered a twenty from behind the plastic pen holder in his shirt pocket, held it out for Kettle, who pilfered a glance at his face. Denbow said, "This is all so crazy, the whole damn thing. That boy never gave me five minutes worth of real trouble in nineteen years, I swear."

"It was a fist fight, wasn't it…to start with?"

Denbow nodded, puffed out a breath. "Over a girl. The other boy had the best of him." He shook his head. "If there just hadn't been a rock handy…my God, why did there have to be a rock right there on the ground? Why did it have to kill him?"

"Don't matter now." Kettle fished a fresh cigarette from the crumpled pack in the top pocket of his overalls, lit it with a Zippo, its silver finish worn to near white. "You said you wanted particulars about life in the big house."

"That's right."

"Surely you've heard things…from other people."

"Some…but I know they held back."

"Maybe I will too."

Denbow slowly shook his head, fingered the sweat gathered under the frame of his glasses, then reset them. "I don't think so."

"What will they give him?"

"He'll do fifteen to eighteen, minimum, the lawyer figures. Says this judge likes big numbers. Plus, the dead kid's family is…like the papers said…prominent."

Kettle drew hard on the Camel; an eighth of an inch turned to orange then died to ash. "It's the sex thing, ain't it?"

Denbow lowered his head, waited.

"They'll be after him. He'll just have to live with it, at least for a good while."

"It's *what* he'll have to live with, Kettle...it's the *exact what* that I have to know."

Kettle squirmed, said, "There ain't no point in it...just ain't."

Denbow turned from the steering wheel, glared a hole between Kettle's eyes. "Listen, you ex-con son-of-a-bitch, I gave you hard cash for a few minutes of your damn time."

Kettle did not blink, and without looking, flicked the cigarette out the window behind him, leaned to within a foot of Denbow's face. Something red passed through the center of his brain, hot and quick.

"So, you want your money's worth, huh? Then listen up, daddy. Judgin' from the looks of you, your boy ain't got a feather on him. That's "hair" to you citizens, understand, and it ain't good for him...and bet he's nice and white-skinned like you too. Which all means that if he's lucky, the biggest, baddest bastard in the joint will claim him for his own little bitch, 'stead of bein' passed around...which might even happen anyhow if his owner's got return favors stacked up...and after his asshole splits and bleeds, he'll get a break while it heals and only have to suck cocks till he's good to drop his pants again. He'll cry and beg the first few times, but that only makes 'em hornier, so he'll learn quick to grit his teeth and make his mind go somewheres else. And he'll lose weight and his eyes will look like piss holes in the snow... and one day, say a year down the hump road, he'll think of hisself as something he never dreamed he could be...and he'll just get over it…or maybe not…and they shuffle him off to the nut ward…but they don't do that easy since so damn many cons are…well, you know, *cons*, and could make a priest believe they're first fuckin' cousins to Jesus hisownself, just for the sport of it."

Kettle fell back against the seat, his chest heaving, sweat burning his eyes. He swiped them with the heels of his hands before snatching a blue handkerchief from his back pocket. He mopped his brow like a man trying to scrub away battery acid. It had all come out in a great rush, too much, too quickly. He looked at Denbow, and it was then that the heaving sobs began to rack the pale man, and after a few, the sobs weakened into steady, childlike weeping.

Kettle fumbled in his top pocket for the twenty tucked behind the cigarette pack, and as he slid from the seat he tossed it behind him.

Helen Puller poked a finger into the window blinds, made a peephole, and watched the beam of headlights probe the darkness, illuminating the driveway. Her beehive permanent was neat and dark, her features winsome. A missed streak of night cream glistened whitely on her cheek. She wore a light green nightgown and terrycloth house shoes. She turned to her husband, who was dressed in brown slacks, black wingtips, and a white short-sleeved dress shirt open at the collar. Don Lee Puller was fifty-eight years old, his neatly trimmed hair flecked with gray, the long furrowed brow hovering over weary grey eyes. His wife glanced past his shoulder at the wall clock, the minute hand five black ticks from ten o'clock.

"It's him," she said, unable to disguise the irritation.

Puller nodded, cleared his throat. "Go on to bed, hun."

"Lord knows, I do have pity for him...it's just...that family hasn't been regular at church since I don't remember when...and now, with the trouble, you're their pastor again."

"That's the way it works out sometimes. I hope to be of comfort, that's all that matters now."

"I know...I know...I shouldn't feel that way, and deep down I don't really. I can't imagine what they are going through with that boy."

She came to his side, brushed his cheek with a kiss and squeezed his hand, slipped away.

Puller waited for the soft knock, opened the door, said, "Come in the house, Edwin." He extended his right hand and Denbow took it mechanically without meeting his eyes. Puller motioned toward the small couch and they sat down on opposite ends.

"Been a while, preacher."

"No need to go there, Edwin. I'd be honored to help any way I can. I have been praying for you and your family."

"I came...mostly...for advice on higher things. My mind is a tangle just now. Tomorrow, at the sentencing, I'm gonna hear the judge put my boy away for a long time...in a place like Hell on earth." He looked at Puller, then back down. "My boy is nineteen, preacher, not strong in any way on earth... not a single way. Do you know what that means?"

Puller rocked forward, clasped his hands together, felt a weight descend on his shoulders, then penetrate him. "He needs to turn to the Lord for help there, Edwin, for the strength he doesn't have on his own. That prison has many men who have done that, and he can do it too. You...me... we can help him do that, help him find the ones who try to live decent."

"Figured that's what you'd say."

"I don't say it idly, just to make words. I've been a pastor since I was twenty-one, and I've seen people...and young ones too...deal with about anything you can imagine."

The room hummed with a lingering silence that filled the ears of both men. Denbow said, "I'll bet you never dealt with a teenager who had been turned into a woman and bled from his bottom."

Puller clenched his teeth, prayed silently for guidance. "We've all heard bad stories, but..."

"They're not stories...just life in the pen where the strongest rule. No use in trying to cover it over. You know that." He waved a hand in futility, closed his eyes, shook his head.

Puller said, "Edwin, he'll just have to cling to the Lord and his family. There's just no other way to lead him...to help him."

Denbow looked up, tears spilling from the outside corners of his eyes. "Now I lay me down to sleep, I pray the Lord my soul to keep." He tried to smile, could not. "I remember the sound of his squeaky voice praying that, preacher. I want now for him to just lay down to sleep, and have his soul kept...just skip the rest of the years."

Puller raised his head, drew in a labored breath. "Edwin, we can't deal with the times and places of a man's passing. Only God knows the appointed hour. There's no use in worrying over that."

" 'The appointed hour' you say. Seems to me that people pick their appointed hours pretty often, preacher." He paused, said, "Is it a mortal sin for a man to want his son's death?"

Puller listened to the sound of his own breathing, felt the throbs of blood crowding his head. He raised his hands above his knees, placed them back, said, "It's not for me, or anybody, to say what is or isn't a mortal sin."

Denbow said, conversationally, "But you're a preacher, closer to God Almighty than me."

"If I am, it's only because I seek to be. If he's further from you than me, that's only because you don't seek him as hard."

"You might be surprised at how hard I've *sought* him in the last few days."

"Then you must keep seeking. Let's drop to our knees right here, Edwin, and go to him together."

Puller began to slide forward, but Denbow stopped him with a knife-like hand motion between them. "No. I've already done that till my knees are sore."

"But, we need…"

"I'm past all that now. Way past. The thing…the one thing I prayed to hear…the one thing…was just a speck of hope back that he might not be used like a piece of meat. I didn't get back one little speck, preacher, and I tell you true, my boy cannot survive down there." He turned to Puller, waited until their eyes met. "I said I came here for advice, but that's not the whole truth. I came for something else too. There's a fancy word for it that wouldn't come to me at first, but I dug around in the dictionary and found it. You know what it is, don't you, preacher?"

A cold hole opened in Puller's gut as the word resounded in his head: *absolution…absolution…absolution…*

The silence thickened again, deeper now, its thrum alive in the close air of the room. "You've got to get this out of your head, man…you can't even think seriously about…"

"I said I was past the thinking now. I've been through it all. My boy will never spend a minute in the pen in Jeff City. Maybe…absolution…isn't really what I'm asking for. Maybe that's not fair to you…reckon it isn't. But if just one high

Christian man like you would tell me that they understand, it would mean more than you'll ever know."

Puller shook his head, stared at the wall, saw nothing. "This...this is crazy. I should call Titus Hood the minute you drive away."

"But you won't call the good sheriff, and you know it, and I know it. " Denbow's smile was thin, rueful. "And God knows it too. Isn't that something, preacher...that he knows too."

Denbow stood, straightened his shoulders. "I find peace in that. You keeping this secret for a few hours...you're really telling me that you do understand. A preacher knows, and God knows, and neither one is gonna throw my boy to the animals." The hard lines around his mouth melted away and he smiled softly. "I know that you'll never think on that as divine...can't ever use it in a sermon...but it must be damn close."

He walked to the door, wrapped his fingers around the knob, then turned back. "I know you're mad at me, and you have every right, but I didn't come here to use you." He paused, lowered his head. "You and my boy will make it across the river, preacher, I have no doubt. Me? Don't think so. But over there in the sweet bye and bye, you remind him how much I loved him."

Puller felt the tap on his shoulder, had no memory of Denbow leaving. He jerked his head around and looked up at his wife, blinked like a man awakening from a nightmare. "Don Lee, are you all right?"

Puller saw in a flash the crossroads looming ahead, realized that the woman linked to him for thirty-seven years—yet a woman guileless—must be led down the easier road. He would have to be very careful; there was no margin for error.

He turned his head around, blinked away the wildness in his eyes, motioned for her to sit with him.

She cradled his right hand in hers. He said, "Well, it was a rough patch, hon, no surprise there." He squeezed her hand gently, willed his features into the grim, useful smile that had served him well for a very long time. "I'm sure…he left better than he came. A long ways to go, certainly…but…better than he came."

Denbow remained awake in bed until the hall clock chimed a quarter past two, and then slipped from the bedroom. The house was still. He padded the ten carpeted steps to the open door of his son's bedroom, allowed his vision to adjust to the faint offering of moonlight, and peered at the tangled form of his wife. It was a sight now burned into the insides of his eyelids, and sometimes he could see it even with his eyes open—a scumbled overlay in shades of gray— the stuffed panda bear clutched in one arm, the bedding helter-skelter from her thrashing. The pattern varied little: she would remain asleep now for the better part of an hour, and then her thoughts would creep from the netherworld of dreams and scratch her awake like talons on her flesh.

Denbow walked to his tiny study, once a pantry to the kitchen, and flicked on the lamp at the corner of the old rolltop desk. He opened the top right drawer, fished through the clutter until his fingers touched first the scissors, and then, farther back, the hand towel and the hardness wrapped within it. He sat the scissors and the dense lump on the desk, unfolded the towel, stared at the blued-steel sheen of the Smith and Wesson snub-nose .38 revolver. The trigger pull was liquid, and he watched the cylinder carefully, noted that it rotated counterclockwise as the hammer rose and fell with a solid, metallic click. The cartridge box was in the opposite drawer, and he retrieved it, plucked out two rounds. He flipped open the cylinder and slid the cartridges in place, then latched it, positioning the cartridges one chamber to the right of the hammer. He placed the gun on the corner of the desk.

With both hands, he slid the chair out, sat down, opened the lower right drawer and looked at the inch-high, gold embossed lettering: HOLY BIBLE. He lifted the big, leather-bound book and pulled the zipper around the edges before placing it open on the desk. He picked up the scissors and began the methodical process of cutting out the pages, a quarter inch of thickness at a time. Within a few minutes the neatly stacked pages lay before him, and he gathered them up, tucked them back into the drawer, closed it. He picked up the revolver and slid it against the page stubs, and then loosely wadded the towel around the perimeter of the gun, careful to leave the grip exposed. He zipped up the cover, poked at it until he was certain of the necessary fullness. The practice went well; with only four trials, he confirmed how easily and inconspicuously he could slide the zipper, secure the grip, and jerk the gun into service.

Denbow sat the Bible and the gun aside and then quietly tore a page from a yellow, legal-sized notepad. He picked up a ballpoint pen and thumbed it open, began to print in precise block letters.

Our boy is free now and it was the only way. Neither one of you could have survived the pen. I hope that you can make another life, but I know it will take a long time. Look around when you are at the cemetery and see how the land heals over. It will be the same for you. You should get a job of some kind and that will likely help—new people and friends in time. The house is only $4,700 from being paid off and

there is still about $3,000 in savings. The lawyer will have to work with you on his bills, but the suicide clause in the life insurance policy has expired, so that's $20,000 to you. And that is none of the lawyer's business. You will be fine on the money.

I know that I have given up the right to ask for anything from you, but I am and I apologize. Could you see fit to bury us beside one another? I certainly understand if you do not want to. I do not want a service for myself and maybe that will make it easier for you to lay us together. The boy first, then a couple days later just have the funeral people slip me in. You could even wait a long time for my stone and it should be a very plain one—flat with the ground. The boy's will be real nice I know.

I feel a certain peace about our son, but can't say the same for me, since I have done this. I do feel some peace for me but I can't explain it. If the preachers have it right, I am in hell. If the unbelievers have it right, I am nothing, the same as if I was never born, but I cannot make my mind go there. I could even be in heaven, who can say really? I have heard said that it is a long road to heaven but a short road to hell. I am hoping it is the other way around. I can't let that go altogether. Well—enough of that. It is over now for me whatever comes. I have been sorted out.

I love you. Or should I say—loved?
Edwin

Denbow, dressed in his best black suit and tie, stood beside the kitchen table, listened for the sound of his wife's footfalls. He looked down at the coffee cup in his steady right hand. It was a positive harbinger, his breathing deep and calm as he drew the brown aroma into his nostrils. The final chain of events had begun.

He heard the soft footfalls now, looked up as she entered the kitchen. She had lost weight that she didn't have to lose, and her once pretty features were drawn and weary, the remains of her figure swallowed up in the light yellow print dress, the little black purse clutched in bone white fingers. Denbow had no clear memory of anything other than coffee or chicken noodle soup entering her mouth for weeks.

"Will they...let us hug him...be...before they take him away?"

"Yes, Ruthie, they will. I was told by the Sheriff himself that we would have a minute with him before they put him in their car."

She nodded, walked to the door and waited for him to open it. He closed the door behind them and led her to the little Ford parked in the driveway. Before he swung her door shut, he leaned in, said, "Back in just a second."

He retraced his steps to the kitchen, then on to the desk in his study. From under a stack of papers he retrieved the folded yellow sheet of paper, walked quickly to his son's bedroom. The stuffed panda was in the middle of the made bed. He leaned down and tucked the note under the faded blue neck ribbon, then returned to his desk and took the Bible cover from the drawer. His wife paid no attention as he opened the rear door and placed it on the floor board. The engine sputtered to life, idled back, and then the car rolled down the driveway.

Don Lee Puller, a moth near the flame, stood ensconced in the mid-morning shade of the ancient bur oak that reigned over the Moniteau County courthouse lawn. He had slipped into position a few steps behind the small gathering of onlookers, the point person for which was a reporter dispatched from Jefferson City whose white fedora bobbed up and down with his pacing. A boxy, black camera with a silver flash attachment was slung over his shoulder. Puller saw the hat stop, the wide brim aimed at the top of the courthouse steps. The boy, head down, was dressed in light blue denim jeans and a chambray work shirt, his hands cuffed in front of his body. Hair like corn silk brushed his pale brow in the zephyr curling around the old building. He had the face of a lost and terrified child. He was wedged between Sheriff Titus Hood and a deputy—big, sturdy men in brown uniforms and tan hats—who loomed over him like a father and an uncle shepherding their pitiful young kin. Hood's ruddy visage was framed by long gray sideburns that matched a wooly moustache drooping over his mouth. Like bloodless incisions, crow's feet radiated from the corners of his eyes. Save for his uniform and the style of his hat, he would have appeared the same to onlookers gathered a hundred years before. They descended the steps slowly, the boy's elbows cradled in wide, square hands. Denbow followed a few steps behind, arm-in-arm with his wife.

Puller's gaze fell on what he first believed to be a large, black notepad tucked under Denbow's free arm, but as the small group drew closer, the preacher blinked twice, and squinted. Denbow was still in sunlight, and before he reached the shade, Puller saw the glint on gold lettering, felt the glad little flip in his chest. Puller made his way around the knot of onlookers, now clearly saw the Bible. With a quarter turn of his head, Denbow looked squarely at Puller, then quickly and discreetly raised the tucked Bible a few inches as he smiled softly, nodded his head in assurance that he had listened to his better angels and turned away from his temporary madness.

"Praise God...praise God," Puller said under his breath.

The little procession shuffled to a halt ten yards from the patrol car parked at the end of the sidewalk. Hood and the deputy carefully guided their charge as they reversed directions, and then in unison took a single sidestep. Hood motioned to Denbow, who whispered to his wife before she walked to her son and gathered him in her arms.

Puller continued to walk slowly forward and was now within ten feet of the family, the welling in his breast a cascading admixture of shame of a cowardice now washed away, and new hope, and of sorrow born of the soft weeping of a mother and a child. *It will be well in time... much time... but it will be well with their souls.*

Denbow stepped forward, placed his Bible hand on his wife's back, tucked his head next to hers, and wrapped his free arm around his son's back. As one, they rocked gently as the seconds collected into a minute. Denbow ran his hand over the top of the boy's head, patted it firmly, began the process of separating mother and son. He whispered in her ear, gently pulled her away, and then guided her in front of Hood as both of his hands took hold of the Bible. It was when Denbow turned back to the boy that Puller saw the the Bible drop, then saw the gun, felt a rending claw in his gut that produced the cry in his throat that would never be loosed. Before the deputy could raise his hands to waist height, Edwin Denbow's left hand clamped his son's head against his own and he fired a shot into the boy's head and then one into his own.

They slumped to the sidewalk like air-filled caricatures of humans, instantly deflated, and only the revolver made a sound that no one heard as it clattered on the concrete before tumbling to the edge of the grass. Puller, mouth agape, was on his knees, arms outstretched as if to catch the fallen pair, now a lump of black and blue. He struggled to his feet, willed his legs to stop shaking. The boy was stone dead, but Denbow's right leg twitched spasmodically, his black wingtip churning on the concrete as if a chamber in his brain now doubted, and sought a saving toehold in a graying world. The twitching slowed, then stopped. Blackish blood oozed like oil between his splayed fingers. A woman's scream ended the surreal silence, but it was not Ruth Denbow's scream. With it came a frenzied whirl of sound and color—brown uniforms and shouted commands, and other, lesser screams and the popping of flashbulbs. But Ruth Denbow had already turned away, had begun a slow, soundless twirl, her fingers opening and closing like a child's futile attempts at catching fireflies in twilight. Puller wrapped his arms around her, felt her delicate weight collapse against him, and he eased her down to the lawn. He looked into her eyes, searched, found no light.

Hood, the brim of his hat clamped in kneading fingers, squatted beside them now, his wide chest rising and falling like a bellows. He looked at the woman, shook his head, clenched his jaws, said, "She's gone from here, ain't she, preacher?"

Puller nodded.

Hood banged the hat on his head, but immediately snatched it off and dropped it beside his boots. He said, mostly to himself, "How in God's name did he do that? My deputy swears his hand never went in his pocket. In all my years...my God...nothin' close to this has ever happened under me."

Puller said, "I'm taking her home to my wife. I'll call you when she can talk, but she won't be of any help in all this, I guarantee." He paused, said, "Help me get her up." Together, they lifted her to her feet, but her legs were lifeless, and Puller swept her into his arms. "Look in his Bible, Sheriff. That'll be the end of your story."

"What's that supposed...to...are you sayin'..." Hood muttered unintelligibly, swiped his hat from the grass and stomped away.

Two hours later, Puller stood on the front porch of the parsonage, saw Hood's patrol car turn the corner and roll toward the house. He walked back inside, through the living room, and peered into the guest bedroom at the two women, now on their feet. On the bed were crumpled, scattered tissues like white Iris flowers dumped from a used bouquet. A large half empty mug of coffee sat on the nightstand.

Without looking up at him, Helen said, "Ruth wants to go home now, pastor, and I'm going on over after a bit and stay the night with her."

Ruth spoke just above a whisper. "Please...not later. Now."

"Sure, dear...right now is fine," Helen said. "The pastor can bring my things over later." She looked up at him. "She understands that the Sheriff has to talk to her and she's all right with that...but there's not much to tell."

Puller took a couple of steps toward them, stopped, and clasped his hands. "He won't be a bother, Ruth. You can trust me on that."

The low rumble of the car engine drifted into the room, then stopped. Puller followed the women through the living room and onto the porch.

Hood stepped out of the patrol car and glared at the dark green Chevrolet Corvair parked fifty feet down the street. He waited until his deputy stood beside him before speaking quietly. "You go tell that fellow—word for word—that if he's still there when we get back I will jam his camera so far up his ass that it'll make a picture of his tongue."

"Yes sir."

Hood's boot sole tapped the first tread of the porch steps as the Chevrolet engine cranked, and before he reached the deck of the porch, the car disappeared around the corner of the intersection. Hood took off his hat, nodded to Puller.

Puller said, "Sheriff, if you'd allow, Ruth wants Mrs. Puller to accompany her from here on, and she understands you have to ask her a few routine questions alone. Hopefully, at her house."

"Why, yes...certainly. That'll be just fine." He turned his head toward the deputy, who stood halfway up the sidewalk, said, "Harold, come escort the ladies to the car."

Hood waited until they were near the car, then said, "You know, preacher, I won't lie to you. This whole thing hurts my pride some...makes me look like a country hick lawman. That's what all the city people will figure...but..." He inhaled through his mouth, carefully repositioned his hat, pushed the air from his lungs. "I got a grown boy...like you...and I know I can't make it right, what Denbow did...but...even if I had known to be suspicious and managed to stop him... can't say for sure...but I think I might feel worse than I do just now."

He looked at Puller, waited for a response, and after several uneasy seconds crept past, lowered his head and turned to leave.

Puller reached out, stopped him with a touch on his bare arm. "None of this is on you, Sheriff. There's no way *you* could have known."

The word hung in the air, resounded like an alarm bell inside Hood's head. *You...you...you...*the little word that should have been lost in the absolution, but was not. Like a warm beam against his forehead, Puller felt Hood's gaze, and he swallowed, the tip of his tongue parting his lips as he looked up. The secret had been spilled by the cadence of a single syllable.

Hood said, "Well then...that clears up a couple of little puzzles for me. I called my wife and she tells me that Denbow wasn't much of a church man, much less a Bible toter...and you being there. Well..." He drummed his fingertips on the handrail. "We'll be laid in the bone yard, you and me, preacher, before we ever speak of this thing again if I have my way, but I just want to know one thing. Were you there to stop him or to watch?"

Puller lowered his head, looked away. "May God forgive me." He turned his head back toward Hood but did not look up. "He came here last night, told me his boy would never spend a minute in the pen. Then today, when I saw his Bible...saw him smile all brave at me...I took it as a sign that he had let it go, would try to help the boy make the best of it down there." Puller shook his head, said, "I did not know about the gun in his Bible, but that does not take away my sin."

"Then it wouldn't have mattered a whit, even if you'd tipped me off. I would have checked his pants pockets and his suit coat...but that big old Bible...huh uh, no way." He paused, furrowed his brow. "I'm sort of an expert on sin... even carry a name after a book in the Bible. But I'm expert on the practical side, not the Bible side. I've seen about all the varieties of sin people can come up with. And yours, if it is one, don't amount to a hill of beans. Denbow and his boy? If old Saint Peter turned them away at the pearly gates...well then, I say most all of us are in real deep poop, and to hell with it all."

Hood slid his fingers along the handrail as he stepped down to the sidewalk. He looked across the street at the church building and the tall white crucifix atop it. "I know that ain't much comfort for a man like you, but it's all I got for you. Any more...you'll have to cross the street for that."

This is a story that might never have been put to pen, but for a casual conversation that I had with a friend who long ago was an extraordinary baseball player. The events are true, with only name changes. I have taken some license with dialogue in order to recreate scenes as my friend remembers them. I was almost angry with him after hearing the story, the thought of it being buried with him nearly repugnant. He told me that he kept it to himself rather than thinking that others would likely consider him either braggart, or worse, an outright liar. I told him that anybody with an IQ in double figures would know that it couldn't be made up. In the end, it is a sad story, at least to me. And I know it is for him.

ANTHEM FROM THE BLEACHERS

Children wish fathers looked but with their eyes; fathers, that children with their judgment looked; and either may be wrong.

William Shakespeare

I believe that the path was set in solid stone for both of us when my father was twelve or thirteen—going on thirty, like they say—covered in meat blood, wrapped in a heavy rubber apron sized for a man, wet stench in his nostrils, in the bowels of his German-immigrant father's butcher shop in Union City, New Jersey. I can see him there under a huge, naked light bulb, his breath frosty smoke, like a child actor in a grainy black and white movie reel, flopping a beef quarter onto the steel cutting table, hacking away at the red mass, the cold blade edges marking his numb fingers as he cleaves away his youth. He spilled his memories carefully, purposefully. The forefinger and middle finger of his left hand were tipped with tiny claw-like nail remnants that had risen stubbornly from nail beds not quite destroyed by the cleaver whack that had shortened both fingers by a half inch late one afternoon when fatigue, always the silent enemy, won a skirmish. "My father soaked my fingers in kerosene while he told me that this would serve as a good and easy—since it could have cost me half a hand—lesson about not paying attention when I got tired, and then my mother made a poultice. I wet myself, but I didn't cry. I missed the next day of work after school, but I wasn't allowed to miss any school."

What the vast majority of immigrant-parent kids did in the early nineteen-thirties was to trade their childhoods for the opportunity to grow up and do something—any damn thing—that allowed them to bury with their parents the memories of butcher shops and sweat shops. But my father was not of the vast majority. For him, it would have been an utter waste, if not outright sacrilege, to bury useful lessons about any aspect of life. I think he considered these snippets from his past like antique but still sturdy tools in an attic box, the lid closed but never locked. They served their purpose. I understood.

When World War II consumed the country, he enlisted in the Army Air Forces and gave up two years in the European Theater, surviving thirty-four missions, for endless, freezing hours scrunched down in the tail-gunner position of a B-17 Flying Fortress bomber shooting .50 caliber bullets at the fighter planes of the German war machine—a monstrosity that served to cancel any latent ties to the land of his father's birth. I doubt that many remained, given family accounts passed down about my grandfather's last months on earth. A first-generation German immigrant and a proud United States citizen-soldier, Grandpa had lived the hell of the World War I trenches in France and had survived a German mustard gas attack, but not without paying the dreadful price of a wheezing rattle that tortured his lungs for the remainder of his life, finally filling his death room with ghastly, wet gasps that chased away everyone but his stoic wife. American citizenship was a gift from Grandpa and my father as well. That, I understood too.

After the war ended in 1945, he married my mother, and a year later I was born. He took a low-level job at Western Electric, and I know it was then that the rage to rise higher—whatever the hell it took—grew in his belly like me and my brother and sister grew in Mom's belly, and he slaved his shifts and went to night school on the G.I. Bill at New York University until he had earned two degrees in mechanical engineering. He slept five hours a night, maybe. From wallowing in the blood of animals to a respected engineer with Western Electric. Nine hundred ninety-nine times out of a thousand, you hear somebody chirp, "blood, sweat and tears," it's silly horseshit. My old man was number one thousand. May be that I've told you the end of this story even before it begins, but it must begin with him; otherwise, you would never understand how he took something precious from me without even knowing that he had. You would never understand why I hate his memory, but not him.

Give or take a week or two, my twelfth birthday in July of 1958 marked the date when my kid's brain registered the certainty of it all: I was better than everybody else when we set foot on a baseball diamond. And I don't mean a little better. I didn't strike batters out, I humiliated them. I made them dread their trips to the plate. They waved their little bats the way a ninety-year-old in a nursing home waves his bony hand at a dive-bombing wasp. Home plate belonged to me, and they knew it, and they knew that I knew that they knew. Word got around. The tall, rawboned righty kid from Cresskill, New Jersey, could flat bring it. When I swapped the mound for the batter's box it was the same story in reverse. If I didn't blister a BB at some poor kid, I'd hit a rocket out of the park. The third basemen and shortstops played short outfield. Even when I got under a pitch, half the time the ball carried out of the park, and the other half it soared so high that the outfielders turned into dancing bear cubs waving gloves. Hell, I must have batted .800. That was also the summer that my father began finding more and more chores for me—productive things—things a boy could begin to build a life on. The foundation was laid for the unspoken law of my youth—baseball was no more than a healthy game to be played when time allowed. He could demand my body, and rightfully so, but my mind wandered where it chose, and that was on the ball diamonds—my little ones, and those a few miles away inside of Yankee Stadium and Ebbets Field and the Polo Grounds. Fields of dreams. With all due respect to Phil Alden Robinson, my fields of dreams were painted on the inside of my eyelids long before he made his marvelous movie. But I never once dared imagine that one day I would actually stand on a dream field, feel the turf and dirt under my spikes, pitch to Matty Alou and Jim Davenport, or mingle spirits with the living legend, Willie Mays, as the crowd roared for me.

Late that summer my Pony League All Star team played the first game of the state championship series without me. The game was scheduled on the last day of a four-day family vacation at my father's sister's place in upstate New York. It was a foregone conclusion around the league that I would open on the mound. Give or take a few minutes or hours, my foresight at that age ranged from about fifteen minutes to a maximum of a couple of days for really important stuff. So it couldn't have been more than two days before we left town when I dropped the bomb on my coaches and teammates that I would miss the opener. "The hell ya say, Dwight! You gotta be shittin' me?!" Heard it a dozen times. Just flapped my arms like a bewildered penguin and shuffled away. At game time, I played whiffle ball with my kid brother in my aunt's scraggly front lawn while the adults passed the time away on the porch munching potato chips and sipping beer, rambling about the same subjects they'd been rambling about for the first three days, and probably for the last twenty years. Turned out that my team scratched out enough runs to cover the runs that I wouldn't have allowed, and we advanced. Next game, order was restored to the world, and I was back on the bump where I belonged and, yeah, it was lights out for the other side—smoke from the mound, wicked shots with the lumber. Pony League State Champs, they called us after that, despite small talk and potato chips on a porch in Syracuse.

Those Little League and Pony League years would have been less than memorable for an oversized pitcher like me had it not been for an Italian father and son team named Rocco and Zani Rizzo that is forever emblazoned on my baseball soul. Reason being that any pitcher, no matter how good, can be driven to maddening mediocrity by a catcher who can't catch him. I'd gotten a bitter taste of it before the Italian tag team came to my rescue, back when the "Little Tyke" catchers turned their heads and poked their mitts in the general direction of one of my heaters, which was a swinging third strike that looked exactly like a line-drive single

STEVEN W. WISE

standing on first, after he'd run down there at his leisure while Tyke was fetching the damn ball. Talk about something that lights a pitcher's ass white hot. But I only got a taste of it, and it just made me appreciate these guys all the more.

Rocco was a fireplug of a guy with a laugh that infected anyone within about a quarter mile. One of those contagious belly-wheezers is what he owned. No way you could hear one of those beauties and not get cranked up yourself. He lived and breathed Brooklyn Dodger baseball—and especially catching great, Roy Campanella—with a consuming passion that was almost frightening to an ordinary ball fan. "Campy", as he was known to adoring fans, had been retired for a couple of years at that time, but the memories of his exploits on the diamond were not retired in Rocco's mind. To this day, I couldn't tell you for sure whether or not Zani's passion rose to his father's level, but it didn't matter, since he didn't have a choice in the matter of pursuing excellence behind the plate. Probably got his first catcher's mitt stuffed into his cradle, his first lesson about how to snap the throw from behind his right ear when he was two.

Rocco found an unused piece of ground at the edge of a nearby subdivision and built the local kids a diamond, complete with regulation base paths, a mound, and a backstop. We'd play two-on-two, three-on-three, whatever, didn't matter. Zani was still getting those back yard lessons in Little League, loud and clear. *"Come on, come on, come on, Zani, snap that pill from your ear like Campy!"* It was like an Italian mantra sung by some wild-eyed guy with a Pavarotti voice, like it should have been scored on sheet music. I can still hear it, can't help but smile when I do. So the three of us labored in love of the game, Rocco hopping all over the diamond like Leo Durocher getting after an ump. In the beginning, Zani was lucky to even get a mitt on my fast ball, and then after he could, I tore the thing to shreds within a couple of weeks. No problem. Rocco came through with a mitt fit for a young Campy, and we were on our way to Little League stardom. Before long, Zani was brass balls back there, I'm telling you. Like I said, he didn't have a choice.

By my freshman year at Tenafly High, the baseball coach lived in constant regret that his ballplayers had to be sophomores before they could join the varsity. He knew the same thing that any baseball person far and wide knew: I could have pitched for Tenafly High—or any other team that they played—when I was twelve. By my sophomore year, my heater had a new companion: the curveball, a.k.a. the hook, Uncle Charlie, the hammer, the deuce, the yakker. Any kid my age that had fiddled with a baseball for a few seasons had figured out how to spin it off of his first two fingers, make it swing sideways a little, but baseball people didn't pay any attention until the ball had some twelve-to-six action—ten times more important when a good hitter was in the box. Curves that move sideways stay on the same plane as a swinging bat, and tend to have line drives attached. I had a twelve-to-six hammer. I was facing juniors and seniors that had some talent, kids that had seen a pitcher with a man's body a few times, but my hook kept them honest. If they weren't looking for the fastball, there was zero chance that they could catch up to one, so when I did mix in the curve I saw buckling knees and steps into the bucket. By the end of my junior year I could count on the fingers of one hand the times that a hitter had centered a pitch, hung out a frozen rope. Might have had their eyes squeezed shut for all I know. Blind hogs find acorns now and then. Cocky, you must be thinking, I know. Hell no, I wasn't a cocky kid, and even now, forty-six years down the road, telling you this gives me pause, but If I'm going to tell you the whole story, straight and true as a foul line, you have to understand what I could do with a baseball when I was seventeen.

My high school catcher was a brute named Rob Trogden. Looked like he could have been a starting tight end on a major college football team. Hunt bears with a dinky hickory switch, and all that. Truth was, baseball wasn't his game, but, God, how his father wanted it to be, and Rob too I suppose. Mr. Trogden was deep into leather and bats and dirt and base paths and Yankee stats just like Rocco was with his Brooklyn Dodgers. I never knew what he did for a living, but what he lived for was to be a part of the battery that was turning heads in our corner of the world. Rob could hit some, but his worth to the team was the fact that he could catch me without fear. I could cut loose with a curve in the dirt even with the rare runner on third, and know that he would stop it. Could have stopped a bullet from a .38 revolver, big Rob, and his father reveled in the dusty beauty of the son squatting in glory back there, his man-child catching the other man-child that every-body wanted to see. Kickin' ass and close to heaven, I know he thought. When I remember Mr. Trogden's eyes—steely love—after a game, his square hands clamped on his son's shoulders, reaching up to gently cuff him on a grimy cheek, I always thought back to Little League and Rocco, and I guar-antee you that both of them thought they saw heaven, or something really close.

I'll never know for sure just how Mr. Trogden got us inside the Polo Grounds. I do know that word got around about big kids who could throw heat at ninety and bend ham-mers from top to bottom, not to mention launch taters out of the yard with the bat—which Rob could do too—and beyond that, catch me smooth and steady. Somehow, Mr. Trogden got hooked up with some baseball people at a very high level. The man could talk baseball like a smooth auctioneer peddling a diamond collection, but there was no bullshit about it; Mr. Trogden knew his baseball. I know it seems crazy that I never made Rob dig around and feed me the details, but you have to remember that we were barely seventeen. We didn't care about how it came to be that a dream got laid at our feet; it only mattered that it was there to be picked up.

It happened in a whirl compressed into a day and a half. On Tuesday, July 16, 1963, my seventeenth birthday, Rob told me that his dad had arranged for us to be a part of a prospect tryout with the San Francisco Giants, who were in town for a two-game series with the Mets at the Polo Grounds. Important eyes would be looking. They'd pick me up at one o'clock the next afternoon. I just stared at him with a stupid jack-o-lantern grin. At the dinner table that night I mentioned the great event to come on the morrow. Mom sliced off a piece of birthday cake as my brother and sister stared at the swirly frosting. She said, "That's very nice of Mr. Trogden." My father nodded, "Humm." That was it.

The ride down to Manhattan was mostly small talk between Rob and his dad. I rode in the back seat and chimed in now and then, but the enormity of the deal was finally setting in: I'm riding to the Polo Grounds because the Giants want a look at *me*. Holy shit, they want a look at *me*. I don't want to talk, just think. I remembered the first time I saw an aerial photo of the quirky old park. Looked like if God wanted a bathtub he could let it rain again for forty days and forty nights and fill the sumbitch up, and he'd have one. Pieces of games I'd watched on TV flipped through my mind, and I homed in on the ball field—the high school distances down the lines, the wide expanse behind the plate and between the infield foul lines and the good seats, the bullpens in the outfield and in play, the forever of centerfield and its cut-out notch to the 483-foot mark. Like I said, quirky, but baseball is a quirky game, and I loved the place from afar, more than Yankee Stadium or Ebbets Field. And now, afar was about to change to real close.

Mr. Trogden had all the wheels greased. He steered his big, shiny Buick into the parking lot near the right center-field corner of the tall white façade like some chauffer delivering baseball royalty, and we all piled out, me and Rob in our high school uniforms, tattered shoes with spikes worn to nubs tied together and dangling from one hand, gloves in the other. Perfect July afternoon in the city—a few monster cotton balls floating against a high, blue sky, a nice zephyr working against the strong sunlight. As we neared the player's entrance, the fans began to drift in our direction. Just before we went in, some kid, maybe ten or eleven, shoves a scorecard at me with one hand, a pencil stub in the other. I shuffle forward, momentarily mystified until it dawned on me that he wanted my autograph. *"You must be shittin'me"* – thought it, but didn't say it. I felt my face redden as I hustled through the doorway and listened to the kid bark his displeasure at me.

Inside the walls there was order. A uniformed coach took charge of me and Rob, and it dawned on me that there weren't any other prospects there—just me and Rob. I'd figured there'd be several other kids who would be getting a look. Not so. Just two kids from Tenafly High headed for the visiting locker room occupied by the San Francisco Giants. The coach says, "This way, guys, come on now…clubhouse door is right through here, then we'll stay in the front part. Leave the players alone." I see faces first, then bodies in various states of dress. I recognize two of the three Alou brothers, Felipe and Matty, and Jim Davenport, and the old man Harvey Kuenn, and Juan Marichal chatting up the spit-baller, Gaylord Perry. They move about in their inner sanctum like gladiators making ready for their entrance into the arena ringed by thousands who will cheer or jeer as they please, and the combatants will deal with it all, triumph or failure, come what may. My memories of these players move over the landscape of my mind, never quite fixed in place so that I might frame a portrait and tuck it away. But two memories are portraits, freeze frames that I can still see with the clarity of an awed teenager. The first is McCovey, the angular giant who stands beside his locker with a bat on his shoulder that looks more like a piece of building material than a tool for hitting baseballs. But the second is even clearer, and I know that I will take it to my grave. It is the sort of vision that might bring a final smile to me on my deathbed. Sure, family will come first, but they will bear tears and visages of sorrow and it will be hard to smile at them. But I hope that energy will remain for Mays, the god of centerfield, the ball player known to millions running like a man possessed as he defies the physics of the blast off of Vic Wertz's bat in the '54 Series. THE CATCH. Stop any Joe Schmoe, anywhere in the sprawling city, and ask him what THE CATCH was, and you'd get an earful in 1963. "Hell, I was there, buddy…" Right, right, Joe, sure you were, just like me and about a million other fans. We were all there, in spirit, and it's okay to lie about that. May someday myself. But it's no lie that I was in that locker room, twenty feet from him, trying not to stare and failing comprehensively. He is bare to the waist, reaching into a box of baseballs that he is autographing. Like the wings of a colossal brown butterfly, the lat muscles ascend from his belt, blend with bunched shoulder and arm muscles that slide beneath his skin as if creatures separate from the man himself. But it is the man that gives them direction and grace and wills them to perform acts that make grown men swoon and scream like children on a wild carnival ride.

Mays. Baseball. The Show. All the same thing, an eternal trinity of the game.

One of the trainers breaks my reverie, holds out a Giants uniform, asks me my cap size and tells me that the long-sleeved undershirt and the cap are mine to keep. I peel off my school uniform and when I'm down to my skivvies, the trainer pops back over, points to the red and purple carnage that is the side of my right thigh. "Good God, son...the hell is that?!" Evidently looked worse to him than to me; pretty much status quo scabby meat from April through September for years. I'm embarrassed, tell him that I slide real hard. He darts away for a few seconds and comes back with both hands loaded. He salves the mess, gently wraps it in gauze, and then hands me a pair of snug-fitting shorts to hold it in place. Before I can thank him for treating me like a real major leaguer, zip, he's gone again like a corpsman looking for another wounded soldier on Omaha Beach. I hold up the undershirt and then bounce it on my fingertips, feel the perfect smoothness of the fabric the same way that I would hundreds of times hence, until the thing finally fell apart at the seams years later. The uniform number is 35, Sal Maglie's old number, but I didn't know it at the time. He hadn't pitched for the Giants since '54, but "The Barber's" number was still fixed in the minds of fans all around the city. He would always be one of theirs, a possession, like all major leaguers who rise to the upper echelons of the game.

I put the uniform on slowly, savoring every thread—the rich, road grey, the dark stripes around the collar and sleeves, the one down the trouser legs, the familiar GIANTS across the chest. I glance across the bench at Rob; he's in his uniform, I'm in mine, and we grin at each other, shake our heads in wonderment. A voice near the ballpark door booms out that it's time to go. We puff out our chests, walk like gladiators toward the arena. We enter the field from the deep notch in dead center and I float across the smooth, green turf, veering slightly to the right so that I can touch the grass where THE CATCH was etched into history. A few thousand fans are already in the park, the home team Mets having finished batting practice, and I dare to look up at them as a smattering of applause breaks out. I get goose bumps like monster pimples on the back of my neck.

The coach lays it all out for us: run some, stretch out and take some long toss, the usual deal. That done, he leads us toward the left field bullpen. He says, "Son, what we look at is your speed and movement, but strikes as much as anything. We expect to see four out of five strikes. Wild don't cut it up here." The fans are within twenty feet of us, and some guy yells out, "Hey, the Barber's back!" I ask the coach what that's all about and he chuckles, tells me about Maglie's old number. My arm feels good, and soon Rob is the magic twenty steps away and I'm humming it, the echo of the pop in his mitt music in my ears. The coach tells me not to try anything special, just hit the mitt like I do in my high school games, work up to my best fastball, a few curves, but mostly the heater. He says, "If you've got good velocity and movement, we can teach you all the rest." I throw mostly four-seamers that hiss in and jolt the mitt, but mix in some two-seamers that would have eaten up the knuckles of a right-handed batter or sailed just off the plate to a left-handed batter. I don't labor at it. I'm lost in the windup, the push off of the rubber, the follow through. I'm in my element with Rob, in the wondrous tunnel-world sixty feet six inches long. I finish up with a curve that bites down and nasty, and a four-seamer that rides up in the strike zone. The coach claps me on the shoulder, the hint of a smile turning up the corners of his mouth. "Nice stuff, kid…nice."

The coach waits for Rob to join us. "Okay, guys, we're gonna go to the mound and you'll get three hitters." He points t me, "then you go to center and shag some," then Rob, "and you get some cuts at the plate." He tells me to throw three-quarters, watch to see if they wanted fastballs or curves. It's awkward behind the L-screen, unfamiliar territory for me, but I manage to throw some strikes to Matty Alou, the little lefty outfielder. Then Jim Davenport steps in, and I cut loose with a heater, pumped up now—the hell with the three-quarter stuff—and buzz his numbers. Boom! He drops like a sack of bricks, gets up and dusts himself off. "Hey, kid," somebody yells, "that was supposed to be a curve!" I think, *"Oh shit, come on, Dwight..."* Rob holds up two widely spaced fingers and sweeps them just to make sure, and I nod. I lick my lips and wind up perfectly, but the ball slides off of my fingers way too soon, right at Davenport's noggin, and down he goes again. A couple of chuckles arise from behind the batting cage, and he turns and flips his bat as he walks away. I should be mortified, but I'm not really. I've already strutted my real stuff. The hell with this batting practice deal, hiding behind a screen and throwing off of some spongy carpet mound covering. It was like chucking rocks over a neighbor's fence at a dog you hated, mostly guessing where the missile would go. I somehow got through another batter, whose name and face are blanks, and I trotted out into centerfield where I wanted to be. The big boys were twirling bats and approaching the cage.

I plant myself in medium center, in a little cluster of players, mostly pitchers, yakking it up, paying just enough attention to keep from being nailed by a liner up the middle. I'm in no mood to be a part of this, consider it basically a squandering of the chance to play fantasy center until Mays did it for real in the game to follow. The fly balls seem to hang forever up against the blue—tiny black dots—real major league flies, mixed in with bullet liners and sharp grounders. I'm watching the big boppers—McCovey and Mays and Jim Ray Hart—as they shuffle around outside the batting cage. I lock onto McCovey as he strides into the cage with his crazy-big lumber. He takes a few easy strokes at first, then, like a machine shifting gears, the balls turn into moon shots deep into the bleachers in right center.

What happened next will always remain something of a wondrous mystery to me, but maybe it shouldn't be. My grey matter at that point in life oozed baseball, because that's all that I cared to absorb. The clarity of my precise location on God's great globe at that moment in time nearly made me dizzy, and I pounded my fist into my glove, cleared my head, watched with hawk's eyes as McCovey waggled his bat. Sooner or later, he was going to smash one to deep center, and I knew that the ball would never touch the ground because I would trace Mays' path and catch it. Swear to God.

The pitch was down the middle, belt high. The ball is in the air before the crack of the bat reaches my ears, and a rush of adrenaline shoots through me like a jolt of electricity. Before the ball reaches its apex I make a guess about where it might land behind me, and turn and run as fast as my long legs can carry me. My chest pounds, my hat blows off, and the longest four seconds of my young life tick away before I peek over my right shoulder to locate the ball. It's falling like a little black meteorite as I make a final lunge with my arm out-stretched and I snag it in the webbing. My momentum carries me to the edge of the warning track at the corner of the center field notch and I can hear the wild cheers of bleacher fans filling my ears and heart like an anthem from Heaven sung by angels, sung just for me. I still wonder if Mays saw the catch, maybe got a chuckle out the crazy kid tromping over his turf. The thought of keeping the ball never crossed my mind; I'd be ashamed to tell you just how much money I'd give to own it today.

The ride back to my house was subdued; even Mr. Trogden seemed emotionally drained. The Mets' announcers rattled on the car radio with their pre-game commentary, the big Buick engine droned smoothly. I was stretched out against the corner of the back seat, Giants cap clamped on my head, floating wistfully away from my field of dreams. Nestled beside my glove was a sandwich wrapped tightly in wax paper. They gave both of us a couple of the beauties in the clubhouse before we left, and to this day, I've not seen their equal. "Stuffed" isn't the right word. Meats and cheeses and pickles and onions, all slathered with mayo and mustard—made the bread slices look silly. I picked it up just to feel again the marvelous density of the creation, and thought to myself, *"So, that's a sandwich in the Major Leagues..."*

Just before bed that evening, my little brother, Eddie, poked his head around the door to my room and said, "Dad told me that he saw you at the Polo Grounds today." I was rendered mute for a couple of seconds as the incredible pro-nouncement settled into my brain. I finally mumbled something at him that I don't remember clearly, and waited for him to leave me alone. I shut the door, plopped down on the side of the bed and reached for a long, black sleeve of my keepsake undershirt, pulled it into my lap. *He was there.* Must have switched trains on the way home and jumped a local line. My father had not uttered a single word about being there to anyone at the dinner table, nor had anyone else brought up the subject. I wasn't surprised; my baseball successes were never the subject of family discussions, and I had already tucked the implausible events of the afternoon into a compartment of my brain, knew that it was mine and mine alone to savor. I was fine with that, until my brother delivered his stunning news. Why had he told my kid brother, knowing full well that the word would be passed on to me sooner or later? Why? I flopped onto my back, stared at the ceiling light fixture. It could only be that he wanted for me to know, but couldn't allow himself to tell me in person, lest I take it as an affirmation—however small—of my rising stature in the world of baseball. Lest I begin to seriously entertain the worthless, harmful fantasy that I could be a big leaguer. Lest I begin to consider skipping college. He stood at the crossroads, feared the path that he had just seen with his own eyes, trusted only the other, paved with sound judgment and intellect.

My father was a brilliant man in many ways, pragmatic to the core, and I had no doubt that sometime within the previous year or two he had researched and run the odds on my making the big leagues. Bet he could have recited down to the tenth of a percentage point just how many high school ball players ended up on Major League rosters. A very skinny number. I remember the little scratch that raked across the inside of my gut just then. I can't tell you that it was the claw of hate, but neither can I say that it wasn't. I rolled onto my side, made a wadded pillow of the undershirt, willed my thoughts back to the sound of my fastball popping into Rob's mitt, the feel of the pitching coach's hand on my shoulder, the bleacher fans singing their anthem of cheers. *He was there.* I wondered then, and still do, if he told anyone around him who he was. Maybe leaned over to the guy next to him who had just sloshed beer on his wrist while he cheered, pointed and said, "That's my boy there, how about that?" Most likely not. But I'll never believe for a second that he didn't smile and join in the anthem. Even I can figure the odds on that, and it's not a skinny number. He sang for me, damn straight he did, but he knew that I couldn't pick out his voice.

I need to tell you about the New York Puerto Rican League, and you need to meet Eduardo "Ed" Sanquiche. Eduardo The Deal Maker, they should have called him. He taught at Englewood Junior High School where Mom worked as a secretary, but the first time I met him, the last tag I would have hung on him was junior-high-school-teacher. Ed was fortyish, skin dark gold, wavy coal-black hair—flat out handsome, pure and simple. He didn't look like the former baseball player he once was any more than he looked like a school teacher; more like a tennis pro leaning in behind some bejeweled, tanned lady as he guides her forehand in slow motion. I hope he was the faithful type, because if he wasn't, the debris of wrecked marriages still litters the city. Ed could smile like Satan and make you believe that he was the Lord's first cousin. Puerto Ricans were designed by God to live and breathe baseball. Think about it. Eternal summers, kids that begin playing with sticks and bottle caps when they're about three, Hispanic passion, desire, athleticism. Baseball is an American invention, granted, but don't tell somebody like Ed that it's America's game. If you do, get ready to walk backwards smelling the guy's breath. Little wonder that he picked up on my baseball story around the school. Not that Mom did any bragging about my exploits. Probably, Ed was squawking one day at lunch about his Puerto Rican League team and Mom said something like, "Oh, my son, Dwight, plays baseball in college." Guaranteed, no more than that, but enough for Ed, who sniffed out any lead, large or small, about ball players that might turn out to be ringers, and especially if they were Anglos unknown in Puerto Rican circles. A league team was allowed to have no more than two non-Puerto Rican players. It didn't take much sniffing around inside baseball circles before Ed and I had that first conversation—approved by both Mom and my father— about joining his team after my sophomore year at college in Kirksville, Missouri. I worked those college summers of course—worked my ass off packing books at Prentice Hall, a major publishing house a few miles from home. My check depended on how many boxes I filled, and I soon became a legend to management at the same time that I became anathema to the regulars, who stayed in a constant state of pissiness because I totally messed with the "normal" packing pace. Just made me pack faster. Anyway, I'm still poor as a church mouse, no car, but either Ed picked me up for the games, or he made sure that I could bum a ride from one of his buddies.

We played our schedule in the Central Park complex of diamonds in an area that the Puerto Ricans had essentially claimed as their own. The level of competition was very high; these guys were players, not wannabes, and several of them— give or take a timely break here or there—could have gotten big league contracts. The breaks never came for these guys, but it didn't dampen their enthusiasm or diminish their skills. They worked tough day jobs for groceries and beer and cigarettes, and I soon found out that they played ball for some money too. By the end of that first season, my worth to the team was apparent, having gone from unknown ringer to regular starter. I ate up a lot of innings on the mound, but also played first base and the outfield. I hit .458 against pitchers who had hops, movement, and wiles. By then, I knew that Ed made some bets on the games. He didn't try to hide the wad of bills that grew in his front pocket after a big win, and I figured that some serious money was on the line. He tried to slip me a fifty now and then, but I wouldn't take it, scared to death that I would screw up my college eligibility if word got back to Kirksville, Missouri. Yeah, yeah, I know. About the same chance of the moon slipping out of its orbit. Maybe I was dumb, but it was an untainted dumb. I did eat some porterhouse steaks that covered the whole platter; I did that real often. We lost only one big-money game in Central Park during all my time in the league. Made me feel like crap, even though Ed didn't let on that it was a big deal. I didn't feel badly for long, because it wasn't a week later that the bill wad reappeared in his pocket and his devil-smile was lighting up his face.

Just how much money was on the line became clear in the ninth inning of an important game near the end of the season. There was a bang-bang play at the plate—good throw from the cutoff man, looked like our catcher had the plate blocked, cloud of dust that looked like a bull had run down a matador in a ring in Mexico City, the whole shebang—and the ump called the runner safe. We go one run down in the top of the ninth. Might as well have been an armed stick-up that emptied the pockets and purses of the spectators on our side of the stands, most notably Ed's. The verbal barrage started behind the chain link fence—fingers jutting through, fists banging dents in it—at about a hundred words or so per second, spoken in the mother tongue of Puerto Rico. The ump, a grizzled old guy who was actually very competent, gave as good as he got, and within seconds, the crowd began to spill around the end of the fence and head toward old ump. Ed was right in the middle of it, hands waving above his head, eyes bugging out. They swarmed around the ump like somebody had poked a stick in a giant hornets' nest filled with Puerto Ricans, and I thought for sure that I was about to witness mayhem at some level in Central Park. I was playing first base, and the hornets and the ump moved as one malevolent body all the way down to the bag—long since vacated by me with plenty of room to spare—then slowly around it, then slowly back to the plate. To my utter amazement, they got it all sorted out, and the spectators mumbled their way back to the stands, the ump banged his face mask against his thigh, pulled it on, and we finished the game. We came back in the bottom of the ninth with two runs and won the game. After that, I no longer wondered about the seriousness of the betting money on the line. Curiosity finally got the best of my better instincts, and after the game I asked Ed straight up just how much money was involved. He looked at me with those steady, dark eyes—not unfriendly—paused for a moment, and said, "Dee-wight, you don't really want to know."

Those were halcyon days, two golden summers that sprawl over my memory in ways that words can't adequately convey. I'm probably a fool for even trying to get you there, but I have to try to get you to San Juan before I tell you about the Giants scout. At the end of that final season, I was selected for the Puerto Rican All Star Team. The roster was made up of the best three or four players from each New York city league team, and the gold at the end of the rainbow was an all-expense-paid trip to San Juan for a week to play against the best Puerto Rican teams, which were basically the equivalent of double or triple A minor league teams in the Major League system. We flew on a Pan American Airways jet, zooming out of JFK International, and sitting down perfectly in San Juan sunshine. They put us up in the Camino Real Hotel and Casino, right on the beach with all of the bikini-clad beauties and high-rollers. We ate whatever we wanted, when we wanted it, kicked at the lapping waves barefoot, drank ice-cold beer, and played the greatest game on earth for the sheer love of it. We played the games hard and gritty—the way baseball is supposed to be played. When the locals cheered for us, it was from the gut, that Hispanic passion I mentioned before rushing out like water from a breaking dam. I even learned how to be a cool Anglo around salamanders in the on-deck circle. Ed pulled me aside before the first game, told me that I had to ignore the little critters scampering all over the place, and especially when I was in the on-deck circle. "You smash one of those little bastards with your bat, I might as well send you back home, Dee-wight. These players...these fans, they figure if a guy can't deal with a salamander, he can't deal with a hook aimed at his ribs, ya know?" I'm cool, I told him, and I was. I only shivered a little the first couple of times one slithered across my spikes. We lost some games down there, but won more than we lost I think, given my memory of Ed's smile. I remember smiling too. A lot. And it was about more than salamanders.

Ed set up the meeting with the Giants scout not long after we got back home. It was on a Central Park diamond, before a game arranged totally for the scout, who wanted a look-see at several of us and a talk with a select few. Ed had told me about him, but I already knew that he was the real deal. Everybody who moved in our circles knew who he was; word traveled at warp speed about the scout who had signed Juan Marachial, among other notables. Ed and the scout drift toward me, talking amiably, Ed's hands dancing in the air the way they always did when he was talking baseball—the only way I ever saw him. They draw within a couple of steps and Ed dismisses himself. We're standing behind first base, near the fence. The scout is dressed neatly in a patterned shirt and white linen trousers. Lanky, maybe forty-five, but I get the feeling that he is older than he looks. Thin, well-trimmed moustache, rugged features, hawk's eyes—if Puerto Rico had gunslingers, this guy looked like one. Even standing still, I imagine him in motion in a baseball uniform—

sinewy, effortless grace, eating up ground like a racehorse on the back stretch.

He talks, I listen. He hadn't come to see me perform; he'd already seen me several times—unannounced and anonymous at the edge of the crowd, his preferred method. It gets down to brass tacks quickly; he is essentially a businessman at this juncture of his life and there are other tasks to which he must attend. The offer is solid: likely five-figure signing bonus, along with steady checks that will cover housing expenses, good food, a little spending money. He makes it clear that I won't stay in single-A ball for long if I perform the way he thinks I will. He stands there, as if mounted on the ball diamond like a statue, a half-smile knifing crookedly across his bronzed face, waiting for an answer. I've already made the only decision I can make—forged in my brain over a decade, waiting for delivery by my tied tongue—but I want to gather him in my arms in a hug that would make him grunt and then join my joyous laughter as we seal my opportunity to reach for the baseball stars. Visions of other kids who had stood before him flash through my mind—eyes welled up, laughing like fools in an asylum, weak-limbed. Then I remember who I am, the fantasy passes, and I say, "Well, if I'm good enough now, I'll be good enough later. I have to go finish college." Other than a slight straightening of his smile, the scout has no visible reaction. We exchange final pleasantries, he extends his hand, wishes me luck with my future. Then he walks away. Forever. I can still feel his hand slipping from my grip. Ed drives me home after the game; we say little, dance around the edges of what is on our minds.

Finally, after he pulled into my driveway, he couldn't stand it any longer. "Dee-wight, baseball, she is a strange thing, ya know, my young friend. Doors open...doors close. Things happen. Maybe you start your college ball next March out there in Missouri and it's damn cold that day and you think you're warm but you're not, and something feels like a string being pulled in your elbow, and you're never quite the same. Shit, yes, you can still blow away the college boys, but when you get back here, the fast ball has lost some zip, the curve, she don't want to hammer down no more…goddamn…baseball, she is a strange thing, like a beautiful, wild woman…she do what she want…whenever she want."

It was the only time he ever swore in front of me. I look out the window, don't want to face him, but I do. "Ed, I know what you're saying and you're right." I look away, stare at the yellow rectangle of light shining from the living room where my father sits in his chair, his throne, listening to the opera. "But there's not a thing I can do about it."

He shakes his head, takes a deep breath, says, "Well, it may turn out okay later, who can say, ya know?"

"There won't be any later, Ed. This is it for me and the league. I can't deal with all this anymore. I'm just gonna play ball in college, just for fun from now on. I'm sorry."

"It's okay, Dee-wight. I think I understand. It's okay." He pauses, taps his fingertips on the top of the steering wheel. "Man, it was some good times, huh." It wasn't a question.

"The best." We shook hands quickly, and I got out of the car, walked up the driveway a few steps before I hear the car door open. I turn around.

"The first game you ever threw for me, bottom of the ninth, sacks jammed, one run lead, two outs, full count. I'm sitting over there behind the dugout, my ass on the line for $2,700, and I'm crazy with the thought that you might throw a curve. You glanced over at me, just for a second, and I'm holding one finger against my chest, banging it up and down, but you throw the damn curve anyhow and fan him. Mother of God, I almost fainted. We never said a word to each other about it after that. You remember?"

"Oh, yeah, I remember. Pissed me off that you didn't think I could get the curve over under pressure."

"I knew then, Dee-wight, that you were the real deal, ya know...a player."

I smile in the darkness, toss up my hand in a final farewell. "Good bye, Ed."

I never saw him again, and if he ever said a word to my mother at school, she never told me about it.

I had one final close-up look at the big leagues—fate, I suppose, if there is such a thing. By the summer of 1969, I had married my wife, Carol, whose brother, Von, lived in Seattle, and they arranged a vacation trip. That was the summer after my first year of coaching high school baseball and basketball in a little town called Lost Nation, in Iowa. It was a contented time for the both of us. I felt good about my first school year, knew that I was beginning a career that fit me well, and Carol was pregnant with our first child. One night that August, Von asks me if I want to go to a Pilots baseball game. Like asking a kid if he wanted a candy bar. Seattle's new team would go belly up two years later, but for a couple of glorious years they were the Pilots, and they played in a little bandbox of a park used by the Pacific Coast League. When we arrived and I see the park, he muttered that it was a shame that he couldn't take me to a real big league stadium. I was delighted; the smaller the park, the closer I could get to the field and the players, which we did from the get go. The Detroit Tigers were in town and we hovered over the railings as I pointed out players familiar to me—pitchers of course: Denny McLain, Mickey Lolich, the lumbering Dick Radatz, Pat Dobson. But I was soon drawn to a tall, sturdy lefty about my age, and I grabbed a program and spied his name: Mike Kilkenny, number 35, same as my temporary number at the Polo Grounds. Ed's voice is in my head, *"Baseball...she is a strange thing..."* I couldn't take my eyes off of him. I studied the way he moved over the outfield grass, like an upright panther, loose and powerful and free. I watched even more intently when he came over to the bullpen, which was so close that I could hear the little hiss when the seams of the ball zipped from his fingertips, and the final, longer hiss just before it popped into the catcher's mitt. It was like looking at a mirror image of my body in a baseball uniform. It bothered me. We stayed for every pitch. The Tigers won, the crowd filtered out into the parking lot, and I figured that it might be a long time, years most likely, before I saw another major leaguer up close. I was wrong, by years.

We decided to leave the car in the lot and stroll around the city for a while. Cottony air, the night lights of a big city, the hustle and bustle deep into the evening—a long way from Lost Nation, Iowa. A half hour passes quickly, and we spy a little carnival, the canned organ music and glaring lights drawing us in. We move along the row of tents, listen to the barkers' sharp voices, and then one singles me out. "Hey, big guy, you look like you might could do this! Gimme a look, big guy!" He's wearing a greasy bowler hat over a dirty-toothed grin, lines cut in his face by the years, garish mismatched shirt and trousers, and he's tossing a baseball up and down in his right hand. You could guess the first part of what happened next, but not the end of it. I plunk down two quarters and he shoves three balls across the counter at me. There are six solid wooden bottles, stacked one over two over three, with the top two rows resting on thin boards, and I know that the bottles on the bottom row weigh probably twice as much as the higher ones. Didn't matter. Zip, pop...zip, pop...zip, pop. The barker's grin vanishes, but is replaced by Von's. I know that the barker wishes he had hidden the giant teddy bears, the ones with silver dollar-sized eyes and wide red ribbons, but I tell him not to worry, I don't want them, I just want to hum his scruffy baseballs and scatter his bottles. He scrunches up his crow face, shrugs. Von whoops with glee, plunks down two more quarters, and I do it again.

It was like I could see big Rob back there behind the bottle rack, squatting like a bear, his mitt beckoning. *"Bring it to me D-wight. This guy wants to go sit down!"* Two more quarters. I do it again. A little crowd has gathered behind me. The guy at the next pitching station has stopped to watch. Zip, pop. The sweet music of baseball resounds even in carny tents. Two young men drift up to his station, and the guy watching gives way to them. Somebody behind me says, "Hey, ain't that Mickey Lolich?" They look different in street clothes, sans caps, but somehow the same as they did a few hours ago on the ball field. Professional athletes in their prime don't move the way ordinary folks move, even when they're just walking around in jeans and polo shirts. Lolich is with Number 35, Kilkenny, my mirror image. The spectators multiply like magic around us in a semi-circle. I exchange glances with Kilkenny as I grin, say, "Let's see what these guys got." Lolich throws first, and he tosses at the bottles the same way that he does to Mantle or an unknown rookie—with craft rather than heat. Kilkenny takes his turn and the sounds return to the zip, pop music. The crowd murmurs with a singular voice, words indistinguishable, but I know what it says: *"Hell yeah now, that's more like it... bring it!"* I watch intently: the tall, lithe body, the way it gathers in coiled energy, the effortless whip of the arm. Zip, pop. Sounds exactly like my music. And I know then, without a scintilla of doubt, that there is not a single athletic attribute that he possesses that I do not.

I could be him, he could be me. I nod to Von; I'm ready to leave. We take a few steps before I feel a hand on my elbow. A man, maybe sixty, jowly face wide and rosy under his Pilots cap. "Tell you what, bud…them two ain't got a thing on you." I smile, huff a little laugh, say, "I was pretty good once." At that moment, fifteen-hundred miles from Lost Nation, Iowa, I let go of as much of it as any man could. No man could let go of it all, even if he wanted to. *"them two ain't got a thing on you"* It was a transcendent moment, and will die only when I do. Fleeting dreams have jagged edges that rub against a man's soul when they finally wing away to wherever the hell they go. I want to weep. I want to scream. I walk away briskly until the murmur of the crowd fades, slowly dies away, and only then do I slow down.

We buried my father in the sharp wind of the last day of March of 1997. Several inches of slushy snow blanketed George Washington Memorial Park in Paramus, New Jersey. Sunlight poked through the clouds from time to time, bright, like the light cast by the huge bare blub in the back of the butcher shop that stood, long ago, twelve miles away in Union City. He was seventy-six, the little claw-like nail stubs folded with the other fingertips over his chest. He had hand-picked his and Mom's burial plots fifteen years before; the main requirement was that they be within easy walking distance of his parents' plot. Another requirement was that the location had to be near the tall monument that presides over the eastern sector of the cemetery. He must have rec- ognized the nobility of the tall granite sentinel that watched over the quiet denizens of earth, secure in the knowledge that it would one day watch over him and his bride and his parents. But he didn't care so much about claiming a piece of the monument to grace his ground; rather, he wanted for it to serve as a location marker that would allow seekers an easy starting point. Sensible, pragmatic, in control, the planner—my father, looking beyond the grave. Dust to dust, but spirits do not die. The final requirement was that the plots had to be near an old Northern Red Oak tree. When a man's father dies, a long string of memories begins to replace his flesh and bones, and to a certain extent, the son can choose and sort the memories as he pleases. But not all. Some refuse to be sorted out, cast away. It's like the way sunlight filters through that massive oak in the summer when a breeze nudges the branches and wide leaves. There are patches of light, but shadows too are cast, pushing aside the light.

This feels like it's where the story ends, but it doesn't. For me it never ends, just evolves—light and shadows, shadows and light—like a vapor swirling along behind me as the years pile up. It's not something that I think about every day, but I think about it often. It won't even end when I'm planted under my own marker tree someday. My children, grandchildren, great-grandchildren—sooner or later they'll all learn the story of my lost dream, pass it down like a dusty family trinket that's just a little too valuable to be dumped at a yard sale after an attic cleaning. They'll keep it, I think. I hope. It's their story too, written in blood, sweat, and tears, but mostly tears.

Baseball, she is a strange thing.

This is the prologue from an unpublished novel that I wrote several years ago. Through the years, I've studied many photographs that brought to life the Dust Bowl. They all claim compartments in my memory with scenes depicting haunted, gaunt figures standing beside battered houses and broken down vehicles, and in the background looms an unholy blackness yet again bearing down on them. "Dust to dust" whispers the Bible. This helps me understand.

THE SHADE OF A WILLOW

Four miles east of WaKeeney, Kansas, June, 1934

"The boy is almost ten now, he's old enough to understand what we have to do."

The shirtless man spoke more to the west wind that he faced than to his wife, who stood a step behind. They both squinted against the reddish haze of late afternoon, and they both wondered how long it would be before the sky again boiled black and angry and covered them with the dust of misery. For months, they had heard warnings about the great dust storms that would surely come if the drought of three years did not end. But it had not ended, and three weeks before, the horror came, turning day into howling night. When the wind abated and light returned, the only escape from their soil entombment was through a window.

The woman resisted the urge to move to her husband's side, knew that he did not want her there. "I reckon he might be, Mason, but I'd still like to take Elias with us."

The man shook his head. "Better this way. We can come get him after we make a start out there."

"Out there...you sure it's the promised land out there in California?"

"I ain't sure about anything anymore, 'cept that it ain't rained enough in three years to fill a damn bucket, and that we're near broke, and that the sky is gonna turn black again 'fore long." He turned his head toward her without seeking her eyes. "And that it's gonna be a hard life out there...least for a long time." He turned his head back to face the wind. "Those things I'm sure of."

The woman swallowed against the burning in her throat, steadied herself with two long breaths. "Well...he's always got along with Sis all right, and John...he...he is a good man at heart."

"This won't be no surprise to 'em, will it? You've told 'em that we're sure?"

"I've told Sis."

"We'll send money soon as we can."

"They don't want money."

"Everybody wants money these days. They just don't want to say it out loud."

With both hands, she reached behind her head and adjusted the band holding her hair in place. The touch of the worn dress sleeves on her shoulders was little more than the memory of cloth. "He's down by the willow pond. You comin' with me?"

"At least we do have a little pond, huh? Long as the spring don't dry up with the rest of this parched ground."

"You comin'?"

"No. You know I ain't any good at such things."

Elias sat at the edge of the mud, a small pile of stones at his side. He did not look up as his mother approached. With a thumb and two fingers, he plucked a stone from the pile and tossed it into the muddy water.

"Can I throw one?"

"If you want."

She squatted beside him, selected a stone, and pitched it underhand into the water. The boy shook his head and huffed at her. "That ain't how you do it."

"Never was much of a thrower, son."

Elias turned to look at her, knew she would be smiling her crooked smile. He remembered when it was even and beautiful, her lips turned up just so. It was the most beautiful smile he had ever seen on a face. It was once so, but could never be again. Sometimes, before he fell asleep, he replayed the hurtful night at the kitchen table—the little piece of white cloth covering her bad tooth, the pliers in his father's right hand, the way her fingers twisted with the handkerchief in her lap as he worked the tooth free—the scenes always unfolding in the same order. But it was her silence that would always remain with him, he was certain, even if the scenes faded through the years to come. The silence—even as the tears slid down her cheeks—the awesome silence against the agony. The same night, as she tucked him into bed, she fashioned the crooked smile that would hide the hole from the world.

She allowed the smile to fade; there would never be a good time to say her piece. "Elias, your pa and me...we've never tried to cover your eyes from trouble...no use in tryin' to do such a silly thing. And now, with these awful storms on us, well, there's just no way to make ends meet out here."

Elias could hear it in her voice; the dread seeped from her, carried on the words as they tumbled from her mouth.

STEVEN W. WISE

He knew what was coming, had known it for several days. He would make is as easy as possible for her.

"Son…uh…you remember how we talked about how it might be best for a while…just a time, mind you…if you stayed with Aunt Ellen and Uncle John, down in WaKeeney, while me and your pa found work out west. Then we'd come get you soon as we could…I just know it won't take long." She nodded enthusiastically, wrapped her arm around his shoulders. "They say there's all kinds of work out there…I just know it won't take long, son."

"If that's what you want, Ma, I'll do it."

"It's not what I want, it's what we have to do for now… just have to."

He nodded, tossed another stone in a high, lazy arc. "It's all right with Uncle John?"

"Sure…sure it is, Elias. He's just fine with you stayin' for a while. Said that maybe you could be of some help in the store."

"I can be good help."

She hugged him close to her body, felt the wispy strands of his black hair tickle her cheek. "Oh, I know you'll do fine, son. We Donners are a strong bunch and you're strong as any of us."

"When?"

"Day after tomorrow most likely. Your pa's got to work on the car some more."

They sat in silence for a minute, watched the ripples from the rock tosses. "Well…that's settled then. I'm goin' on in and stir us up some supper. I'll holler when it's ready."

"All right, Ma."

When she reached the top of the little rise, the woman turned back to look at him. He sat in the shade of the willow, and though she had seen him there many times in the past, the dancing patterns of light and shadow had never before caught her eye as they did now. She decided that this was the picture of her son that she would take with her, and she studied him for long moments, framed him, painted him in her brain, and locked the portrait away. She walked back down the slope, sat down beside him. The boy looked up at her, smiled, offered the rock resting in the palm of his hand.

"Come back for another try?"

"No, son."

"Why then?"

"Forgot to show you something." She circled his shoulders with her arm. "Look up there."

She lifted her head toward the willow branches and he raised his head with her. The wind moved the delicate leaves and limbs to and fro, and for the woman, they were brushes in the hand of God, painting her child with all of the shades of life."

"Now lean back and look at your legs and body. What do you see?"

"Pieces of light...movin' around."

"Yes...light, and what else?"

"Little shadows too...movin' all around."

"That's like a person's life, Elias...some light and some darkness, some good and some bad, some joy and some sadness. Some of both will come to you, same as for everybody on God's own earth. Me and your pa have had our share of both. And I know now it must seem to you like the shadows cover the most of us, but the old willow...he's always movin' in the wind, lettin' some light peek through."

Elias rested his head on his mother's shoulder, looked back up into the swirling leaves. "Never heard you talk that long before."

She laughed softly, hugged him. "Reckon it was quite a speech for me, huh?"

"It was a nice one."

"You remember then, Elias Donner. There's always some light that'll come along and push those shadows away."

"I'll try."

Two days later, a half hour after sunrise, Elias stood bravely inside the white picket fence of John and Ellen Mabry's front yard. As the car chugged down the dusty street, he looked first at the back of his father's head and then at his mother's face as she twisted toward him for a final wave, flashing the crooked smile. He watched until his parents were consumed by the dust. The source of the knowledge that came as he stared into the filmy powder of earth would always remain a mystery to Elias, but the revelation was palpable, like the weight of a winter coat on his shoulders. He knew that he would never see them again. The dust cloud boiled high, rounded and as tall as a tree, and then the image of the willow replaced the dust, but the boy saw only the shade— deep and impenetrable.

After reading the incomparable book about the Iwo Jima flag raisers, *Flags of Our Fathers*, an unrevealed scene kept popping up in my mind. Young Corpsman Bradley found the mutilated body of his best buddy inside an enemy cave, and upon returning home, paid a visit of condolence to his friend's mother. What passed between them one can only imagine, but I have no doubt that a needful lie was told. If ever there was a need for such a falsehood, it was then. It could have gone something like this.

JACK-O'-LANTERNS

How do you change the pictures in your mind
that won't be quiet there
or go away, or go away?
From a song written by Dan Schuffman, who fought in
WWII and remembered too much.

The Marine found his buddy in a Jap cave seven days after the battle for Iwo Jima began, and twenty-eight days before it would end. Strictly, that's not accurate; he didn't really find his buddy; rather, found his body, and—strictly again—didn't really find a body, so much as a lump of naked, tortured flesh that had only days before been his sturdy nineteen-year-old best friend. The fading sunlight, weak and colorless, was without energy, but it served in funereal fashion as it seeped into the cave, bathing the corpse in a soft light nearly identical to that which would bathe the evening mourners three weeks later in a cracker box of a church house hovered over by an ancient green ash tree in Hilltop, Kentucky. It would be a memorial service, not a funeral, for a funeral required a body. Two years would pass before the body was disinterred from the 5th Marine Division Cemetery in Iwo Jima's dark sand and returned to American soil. But those are stories for other tellings.

The Marine knelt on one knee, his fingers white-knuckled around the barrel of his M1 Garand rifle. He had been staring from the jagged sliver of the cave opening for three minutes when the guilt finally overcame the hammer strokes in his chest—as if someone of authority had righteously demanded that he account for his time—and he was obliged to reckon that it had been at least a quarter of an hour even though he could not yet make himself study particulars, save for one: the crudely tattooed MOM high on the left shoulder. But now it was time. The Marine studied the head of his buddy's corpse, now devoid of eyes, nose, and ears. Except for an oddity about the mouth and tongue, it closely resembled the jack-o'-lanterns of their childhood, carved for MOM and left too long on her porch steps in the sunny days of November. At first, the Marine's descending gaze registered other large things—arms wired to a stake pounded into a crack in the rock floor, stretched backward and upward, sharp bone ends peeking whitely through skin, a torso sliced in shallow, black-blooded furrows along the rib cage, legs splayed at impossible angles, toeless feet—but as his gaze ascended, the small things appeared. A little toe on the left foot had escaped the cuttings. The right kneecap bore pencil-sized puncture wounds, and protruding from one was the broken stub of a rifle cleaning rod. Both upper thighs were covered with burn marks from cigarettes, like tiny animal tracks leading to the penis stub. His gaze darted back up to the mouth and the oddity that was not a tongue.

"Oh, Mary, mother of God...oh, Jesus Christ...no, no, no...the lousy bastarrrrds!"

He dropped his rifle, turned away, and retched a jet of partially digested C-rations against the cave wall. He heaved until his ribs hurt, then fumbled for his canteen and swished out his mouth with water. He willed himself to suck air into his lungs, waited for the process to even out, for the whirl of his brain to slow. But with the slowing came the burden, and the Marine could feel the weight of it—a cold, heavy blanket suddenly draped over his shoulders—and he knew that one day in the months ahead he must face his buddy's mother and steel himself in her tiny living room and tell the most important lie he would ever tell. But that was an ocean and thousands of miles away, and he would have to survive to tell the lie, live past whatever lurked for him in the taking of this God-forsaken, black, Jap-infested rock jutting out of the Pacific. *Then. Far away. If I live.*

Only the now of it all mattered, emptying his brain of everything, save for dealing with the body. He would fix what was left of his friend before anyone else saw it, puked at its sight, and in the fixing begin the construction of MOM'S lie. He dropped his rifle, a consuming urgency now in control of his every movement. With his thumb and forefinger, he plucked the penis from the mouth and tossed it aside, but the instant it left his fingers he knew he had begun a sacred process with a mistake.

"Dammit...dammit!...think straight!"

He pivoted on a knee, retrieved the penis and placed it carefully beside him. The twisted wire unwound easily, releasing the body, and the Marine caught the cold weight in both arms. He lowered it, careful to cradle the head in one hand as it touched the floor of the cave. The limbs were stiff and unwieldy, and the Marine grunted under his breath as he struggled to straighten them. He unsnapped his first aid pouch, took out the Carlisle bandage, and then placed the penis squarely in the black patch of pubic hair before covering it with the pressure pad of the bandage. He lifted the buttocks, wound the tails of the bandage around them, and tied them tightly. The uniform was in a clump behind the stake, the boots at the base of the wall, and the Marine retrieved the items. First, the shirt, and it was a struggle—stiff arms and knife-sharp bone ends to avoid and back-handed swipes at the sweat stinging his eyes—and then the buttons, only two to work with, and that was easy. Except for tugging out the cleaning rod stub, so were the trousers; he just bunched them around the feet, lined them up, and worked them up into position. Three buttons remained, thankfully, and then he fastened the belt buckle. Boots last, over the toe stubs, a peek at the little one on the left foot as it disappeared. Laced up, neat, final. He reached for his rifle and disengaged the bayonet, jerked out his shirt tail and cut a long strip, six inches wide, then wrapped it over the eye and nose cavities, tied it securely behind the head.

The Marine picked up his rifle and swung it like a baseball bat at the base of the stake, snapping it clean. He reattached the bayonet, laid the rifle aside. From outside the cave, voices began to drift toward him, unintelligible at first, but American voices, and he thought he heard his name at the end of a shouted question.

He whispered, "We ain't got but a minute or two now… what else can I do?"

The fingers. He could do the fingers. The Japs hadn't chopped off the fingers. He bent the elbows, lifted the hands to the chest, laced the fingers, and it was then that grief pierced him through, his chest shuddering with great sobs.

The Marine heard nothing before feeling the touch of a hand on his shoulder. Then came the sounds, muffled, soft echoes in the cave. Boots shuffling, the rustling of uniforms, rifle butts bumping the rock floor, and then discordant voices of men uttering prayers and curses—"Jesus and fuckin' bastards and Christ and heathen sonsabitches and Mary Mother of God and pieces of shit"—all mingled into a solemn liturgy for Heaven and for Hell, and the Marine knew that they had found the shattered stake and the twisted wire and nine toes and a tongue and a nose and ears littering the floor.

A voice, low and gravely, in his ear. "You've fixed him proper...all you could do for a buddy."

"He was more than that, Sarge."

"Same town, right?"

"Same street...gravel."

"His folks?"

"Just his mom. I never knew his pa...long dead."

"She got more boys?"

The Marine shook his head. "Two older sisters."

"Goddamn...her baby boy."

The sergeant fumbled for his pack of Camels, shook it, pinched out a cigarette with his lips. He rolled it between his thumb and forefinger, made no move to light it. "Well, I know you ain't gonna tell her the truth...and I know you ain't gonna just write her about this...so let me give you some advice."

The Marine nodded silently.

"Have it all laid out in your mind a long time before you go see her. I mean every damn detail, you hear me? You make it up in your mind and then you go over it again and again.

And you tell it out loud to a mirror a dozen times so you won't be surprised at the sound of it."

He paused, stabbed the cigarette into the corner of his mouth, did not light it. "Because, I'm tellin' you, son... you just go blundering up to her without practicing...just wingin' it...your throat all burny...and you'll foul it up and she'll know it." He shook his head. "And there won't be no do-overs."

"I'll get it right, Sarge. I swear."

The sergeant clapped him on the shoulder, then stood. "I know you will." With a flick of his thumb, he opened his Zippo, wheeled a flame to life and lit the cigarette. He turned away, began barking orders to the other soldiers, but the Marine did not hear him.

The Marine rode toward the edge of town in a colorless 1929 Chevrolet pickup truck driven by a man whose mouth was lost in the wilderness of a black beard that draped over the top of his coveralls and extended sideways to the straps. He wore a filthy, brimmed straw hat with edges no better defined than the beard. Thick, corded forearms jutted from rolled up shirt sleeves and linked with great bony hands, long fingers clamped around the steering wheel. When he spoke—a frequent occurrence during the preceding quarter hour—it was as if a voice thundered from a brush thicket, rendering pronouncements on subjects ranging from the habits of prime roosters to a surefire technique for eliminating a wasp nest without being stung. At first, the Marine had been pleasantly distracted from the duty he was soon to perform, the jabbering having reduced it to a flame burning low, like a pilot light at the edge of his brain. But now, with less than two miles of gravel road and a short street between him and MOM, he could no longer lose himself in banality, and the flame burned brighter.

The driver tapped the dash gently with the fingertips of his right hand. "I know she ain't much to look at now, but my oh my, in her day…" He shook his head. "Shiny and blue, 46 horsepower, 194 cubic inch cast iron overhead valve engine… first 6 cylinder, by the way…mercy, she was somethin'."

The driver nodded to himself, and then pilfered a quick sidelong glance toward his rider. The only sounds were the whine of the engine and the crunch of gravel. The seconds collected, created a space in the driver's brain, and he knew the Marine had already traveled forward to MOM's house.

"You say she knows you're comin', huh?"

"Yeah."

"Knows it's today?"

"No…I wrote her it would be middle of November before I got home."

The driver reached up and tilted back his hat. "Well… he was the only one we lost around Hilltop. You and him was the only Marines…one more Army…the Hadley boy, and he come back like you. Three left, two come back…thankful for that anyhow."

The Marine nodded, said nothing.

"Want me to take you clear to the house?"

"No thanks." He pointed through the dirty windshield. "This'll be fine. Need to walk a little first."

"Figured that, I did." He paused, made a sound in his throat. "Me…I druther sandpaper a lion's ass than go talk to her about over there…but I know you got to."

"I do."

"Least you say he died of a sudden. Least you got that… thank goodness."

The Marine drew in a long breath, pushed it past his lips. The brakes of the pickup squealed faintly as it ground to a halt. He reached across the seat, extended his hand and said, "Much obliged."

"Twern't nothin', son. Don't forget your bag in back. So long."

The Marine stood in a small copse of hickories at the edge of town, waiting as the twilight thickened into darkness. A few vehicles rumbled slowly by, and he was careful to stand as still as the trees that guarded him. The shapes of roofs and walls faded away and yellow rectangles of light flicked into view, formed a path to the only two houses that mattered. He picked up his sea bag and stepped into the street, and then began to walk toward a particular rectangle of light. He passed his own house from the opposite side of the street, though not without a long glance. The breeze stiffened, cool and misty, and he allowed the elements to penetrate him, sucked them into his lungs as an offering. He concentrated on the gravelly cadence of his footfalls as the rectangle grew larger, and then a shadow passed through it.

An object, squat and round, leaked into his peripheral vision as he climbed the four porch steps, and he willed his gaze straight ahead toward the door, waged for several seconds the little battle he knew he would lose. He turned his head to the jack-o'-lantern, saw the dark shapes of eye and nose holes, the wide, sagging mouth.

God...give me a break...I'm trying so hard...so hard!

He sat the sea bag on the floor, and then made a fist with his right hand and punched himself squarely in the chest. "Buck up, dammit!"

From behind him sounds gathered—a child's laughter, the excited yap of a small dog, a door closing—and then only the wind again, whooshing around the corner of the house. The fist at his chest loosened, and he rapped his knuckles three times on the door, then swiped his cap off.

The door opened quickly. She placed crossed hands over her bosom, bowed her head for a moment, then reached out and gathered him into her arms. The sobs spurted for only seconds, then she steadied herself with two open-handed claps to his back. "Come sit...please."

The Marine followed her to the couch and they sat with knees angled toward one another. He parted his lips to speak, but his tongue was locked to the floor of his mouth, and he could look only at the collection in her lap—worn hands, ringless fingers, a crumpled apron of faded green.

She said, "I treasure your coming...but I know it's hard. That's why it's treasure." She paused, reached out and patted his knee. "I got iced tea made...course I imagine your momma's got you suppered up good." She smiled.

His lips parted wider as he tested his tongue for movement, and then he stole his first glance at her eyes. Warm and soft, they beckoned but did not plead. "I...uh...well, truth is...uh...I come straight here."

"Oh...my." She fished a handkerchief from the apron pocket, kneaded it with her fingertips. "I'm ready then. I just want you to tell me how it ended for him over there. I've heard said that some don't want to know about their sons... but I do...can't have no peace till I know." She opened her fingers like the petals of a flower seeking the morning sun. "However...whatever...I just have to know the truth."

The Marine inched closer to her, placed both of his hands over hers. "We weren't more than a few steps apart when it happened. Nobody even heard the shot. He just kinda whoofed, reached around with one hand to his back... kinda swiped, like he felt a horsefly light on him...and he just looked surprised for a second. Then he buckled and I grabbed him, eased him down. Wasn't even time to call a corpsman...he just closed his eyes...and that was it. Sarge said it was a sniper, no doubt."

The woman eased her right hand free, raised the hand-kerchief to her eyes, then her nose. "Oh my...thank you... you can never know how much this means to me. I take it as gifts from God Almighty...him passin' like that...and you being there with him. It was meant to be."

He nodded, said, "Yes'um...reckon it was."

She bowed her head again, her body rocking gently to and fro, a hum rising from her throat—faint, yet melodious and sweet—and the Marine recognized the tune as a hymn, though he could not find words to fit it. When she finished, she raised her head and said, "I just don't want him for-got. That's not too much to want, is it? Surely people won't forget."

"I can't believe they ever would."

She sighed, scooted forward to stand, and he helped her up. "Well, listen here now...you get across the street to your ma and pa. I feel half guilty you coming here first."

"They'll understand."

"You staying around these parts?"

"Not long. Goin' down to Lexington to find a job."

She wrapped an arm around his waist, walked him to the door, and they stepped onto the porch. She pointed to the jack-o'-lantern, said, "I carved it special for you two...you boys and your pumpkin carvings. Those were good days."

"Yes'um...the best."

He picked up his bag, walked down the steps and into the street. Her voice chased after him, and he stopped, turned around. "It's still in pretty good shape. You come look again in the daylight. It'll be a nice remembrance for you."

He said, "Might do that."

The old Marine sat tilted to his left in the wheelchair, his eyes closed, but he was not asleep. There was no longer any reliable order to things present or past—faces, names, voices, noises, times, places, events happy or sad, sometimes even the four walls of his tiny room—all of life muted in shape and sound, and now only the little one could order his mind, cause him to see and hear sharply, with a purpose. He opened his eyes, blinked into focus the food tray and the blue plastic plate, saw the uneaten chunk of meat, the pile of mashed potatoes, the dark puddle of pudding. He registered no hunger, ate only when the help came and urged him. Only the little one stirred life, and he was to visit this very evening, of that the old Marine was certain.

Voices in the corridor. One manly and vibrant, reminding him of a voice that once rumbled from his own chest. Another—the one he homed in on—small and delightfully squeaky. He raised his head, shifted his back straight, waited for a sliver of the bright world.

"Hey, Gramps, how you doing?"

"Fair, I reckon...fair." He answered the man, but looked at the little boy. His hair was the color of straw, smoothed over his forehead but poking up in back where his hat had made it wild. Wide-set eyes, beautiful and blue and liquid. Nose still a button, cheeks round and ruddy from November's night wind. A white-toothed smile, wide and innocent and true. The old Marine was alive now, lost in the blue eyes, and he felt the tight muscles of his face work to curve the corners of his mouth upward.

The man leaned over the little boy and said, "Want to give it to Great Grampy now?"

The boy nodded eagerly, held up his hands, palms upward. His father reached into his coat pocket, pulled out a jack-o'-lantern not much larger than a softball, and then placed it in the boy's hands. The boy turned, took two steps toward the old Marine, then said, "It's for you, Great Grampy. Daddy helped me make the face."

The dying Marine felt his smile slide, and then came screams from a cave echoing cold and rocky, and visions that he could not blink away. In his chest he felt a wild fluttering, as if a bird caged within his ribs fought for freedom.

His grandson huffed a little laugh, said, "Not too fancy, for sure, but I wanted him to do most of it...and he insisted it had to have a tongue...so...that's where the Tootsie roll came in." He made a sound, less than a laugh. "First jack-o-lantern I ever saw with a tongue...I...uh...Gramps? Gramps? You all right?"

The wail of anguish filled the room, spilled into the corridor, and soon footfalls pounded over the tile, and then into the room. A black woman, fiftyish and sturdy as a man, commanded the close space. "Now, now, there, my old friend... what's the matter now?" She knew there would be no answer, said, "Let's get him laid on the bed, and I'll calm him down... don't worry."

The little boy was crying, the jack-o-lantern clutched to his middle like a teddy bear. The woman said, "Why don't you take him on down to the soda machine, I'll manage now...just need a few minutes."

The man and the little boy hustled past the soda machine and did not stop until the cool night air curled around them. The man squatted, hugged his son to his chest.

"Shhhh...don't cry...don't cry."

The boy sniffed wetly, pushed away and raised his coat sleeve toward his face, but his father stopped him, placed a handkerchief over his nose. "Blow. Okay, now...that's better. Listen to me. Your Great Grampy is very old, and old folks get all mixed up in their heads sometimes."

"But why?"

The man cleared his throat, swallowed, and then placed his hands over the little hands still clutching the jack-o-lantern. "I can't tell you for sure, son. Nobody can...not even Great Grampy."

Too suddenly, the door popped open behind them, and when the man turned around, a white-uniformed nurse locked eyes with him, her lips tightly pursed. She beckoned with two quick flips of her fingers. The man stood, took his son by one hand, and walked toward her, asked the question with his eyes. With a shake of her head that only the man could discern, the nurse leaned close, whispered, "I'm so sorry." She looked down at the boy, said, "If that's not the prettiest little jack-o' lantern I ever laid eyes on, young sir, I don't know what is. I have a lady inside that would just love to hear how you carved it...okay? Your daddy and I have some things to do."

As they approached the door to the room, the nurse stopped, laid a hand on the man's forearm. "We got him calmed down very quickly...and then..." she smiled firmly, patted his arm, "he just went to sleep. So peaceful...you should be thankful for that. Such a blessing."

The Marine's grandson tilted his head toward the ceiling, drew in a jagged breath, and nodded slowly. "He was quite a man in his day. World War II vet...survived Iwo Jima. I've read a lot about it." He tilted his head, raised his eyebrows. "Had to...he would never say anything about it...even to my dad."

"Hummm...I'm afraid I don't know much about that."

The man shook his head, shrugged his shoulders. "Not many do these days."

My father told me this story when he was eighty-three years old. I had always wondered why there was a distance between him and any dog that he was ever around, even the pointers that he cared for so well and hunted the bobwhite quail with. There never was a family pet of any kind around our house, but neither my two brothers nor I ever really wanted one. Maybe what happened to our father was implanted into our DNA with his seed. Let him tell you the story and then you will understand.

FIDO

To love a dog is to risk peril to the soul.

She was the first dog that I ever loved, and the last. I found her (or did she find me?) in August of 1937, a couple of weeks before my thirteenth birthday. Our union had to have been on a Sunday because that was the only noontime that my father's battered, black Ford Model AA one and a half-ton truck with the canvas covered bed was parked in the thin gravel that passed for our driveway. It was behind the right front tire that I spied her tail—a black and white snake twitching every few seconds. I had in my hand a sliver of ice freshly shaved from a new block. She came to me even as I approached the truck, the tail twitching ramping up to greeting speed as determined by little mutts whose ribs furrowed starkly above their bellies.

I extended the sliver and we alternated licks until it was gone, and then she licked my cold fingers, finalizing the bond. She couldn't have weighed more than ten or twelve pounds, and should have weighed half again that much. Short-haired, the black and white pattern splattered over her right side like someone had thrown paint from a can and scored a glancing blow, inquisitive black eyes, ears folded over by half, legs too long for her body—her ancestry was a canine jig saw puzzle.

She was muttdom defined and she was beautiful. I named her Fido, and retain no recollection of the name's genesis; I think that it was simply the fact that I was a kid, and could name a stray dog as I pleased. That first night after supper, I brought her a chicken leg bone smeared with a dollop of gravy and a shallow rusted pan of water. I saw my mother watching through the kitchen window, but neither she nor my father said anything about the new arrival for a couple of days, when Mom warned that the dog was likely to get run over by the truck sooner or later. I told her that I wasn't the least bit worried, and I pronounced Fido the smartest dog I'd ever been around. We soon considered each other as contemporaries, the only major differences being leg count and my ability to talk, although the latter was no real problem; she talked in her own way with a variety of yips and barks and throaty little rumbles. The first time I trotted around the backyard at dusk catching fireflies, she instantly began to run with me, launching to waist height as she snapped at the yellow flickers. After a couple of weeks, I found some scrap leather in the shed, and with some old shears and thin wire, fashioned a little harness for her that I hitched to a small wagon. I figured that she would hate it, probably act like a tiny hardheaded mule, and I'd resolved beforehand that the experiment wouldn't last any longer than her first bucking. To my delight, she took to it like an old mare. We became the toast of the neighborhood, except for my own home. Every conversation about her that I attempted to initiate was met with either stone silence or a quick shift to other topics.

A dog, a truck, my father, and me: four corners of my early life, forming a box that contains to this day chunks of my spirit. I wouldn't realize it for years to come, but the truck represented the only thing standing between abject Depression-era poverty and the slightly higher form of poverty that families like mine considered as a blessing. My father had a small dray business that was financed by an uncle (at a no-interest payback of fifty dollars a month against a thousand dollar price) who had grown weary of sweat stinging his eyes in the summer and frozen fingers in the winter, but most of all, it was the back miseries that he could no longer tolerate. With the business came the Ford truck and the contract with Missouri Pacific Railroad to deliver goods of widely varying shapes and sizes, all contained in railroad box cars side-tracked for downloading. I had already begun helping my father, despite the fact that less than ten Fidos would have made one me. We loaded feed bags, engine parts, scrap metal, tools, tires, rock salt, appliances, bales for the local woolen mill, tombstones, caskets, lumber, bags of cement, and on one memorable occasion, a case of dynamite.

As we scooted the crate to the edge of the box car floor—about waist height to my father, and nearly shoulder height to me—I pulled my side an inch too far. What ensued took place within the span of no more than three interminable seconds. With a hoarse expulsion of "oh shit!," my father squatted and reached under the sliding crate with both hands in a futile effort to prevent the fall. We both jumped backward as the loudest *whump* I had ever heard filled the air, the dust cloud rising like brown smoke. I will never forget the look of sheer terror in his face as he stared down at the crate. I suppose—although

I never confirmed it—the fact that it was new dynamite, with no real possibility of unstable nitroglycerin, suddenly settled in his brain. He turned toward the open mouth of the box car and leaned on his elbows, his wide chest rising and falling with the bellows of his lungs, and then he adjusted the wire-rimmed glasses that never seemed to be in the correct position. After a half minute, he said, "Son, don't ever get in a hurry with heavy things again." I never did, and there was never another word spoken about the incident. On the days when deliveries were light, he always seemed to have other jobs lined up—some late afternoon or evening hours at the woolen mill, the hay fields in summer, helping with livestock, shingling a roof—just about anything one could imagine a strapping man in his prime doing to put food on the table and buy gas for his truck. If he would have ever straightened the tired comma that was his back, he would have stood about six feet; he weighed maybe one hundred and seventy pounds, but the things he could lift with his long arms often caused me to stare in disbelief.

He was raised on a hardscrabble hog farm in Moniteau County, Missouri, helping his father eke an existence out of mud, shit, barrels of garbage that served as feed, and butchered blood and guts. The only dogs that he ever knew were nameless, half-wild curs that were not so much dogs as vultures—circling and yapping, waiting for the next stillborn piglet, or bloodied testicles, or the leavings of a full butchering. He helped on the farm a great deal, given his father's tendency to hitch up Old Sal and wander down the rutted roads leading to the town tavern.

His only self-allowed pleasure was a couple of dozen cigarettes a day rolled from Sir Walter Raleigh pipe tobacco. A few years before his death, and with a cloud of Sir Walter (he'd switched to a pipe by then) partially hiding his head, I asked him just when it was that he started to smoke. He shot a long jet that had rebounded from the bottom of his lungs, tilted his head slightly, and after thinking for a few seconds, said, "Ummm...I'm pretty sure I was seven." My father was never a child, and that fact was the only thing that allowed me to finally forgive him twenty years later.

The beginning of the end came two months after we found each other, when she began to lick herself. I came home after school one day and my mother, elbows akimbo, stood over Fido at the corner of the shed. As I approached, Fido zipped around my mother's ankles and jumped into my arms. My mother said, "Be careful, son, her rear end is messy. She's in heat." There didn't seem to be anything overtly ominous in her tone; rather, it sounded more like a weary pronouncement. But I heard enough to know that trouble was brewing, and I knew where I would be the next day after school, which was at the door to Doc McCann's cinder block veterinary clinic. He wasn't there, but his wife was. A lank, ruddy-faced woman who was as tough as her husband, Claire McCann quoted a price for spaying at $2.00. When I asked her if I might work it out in chores around the office, she scrunched her face into something resembling a smile and said, "Oh, I 'spect Doc can work out a plan for that." I thanked her profusely. "It's Tuesday...ummm...you bring your dog back here on Thursday, 'bout this time."

I never returned to Doc McCann's office. When I arrived home from school on Wednesday afternoon, there was no sign of Fido. I circled the shed and called out for her, the drumbeat of dread building in my chest with each thump of my heart. I swung open the door and looked down at the little lair I had made for her. The tattered towel was gone, as was the rusted water pan. The sixteen penny nail that I had driven into the wall for storing her harness was bare. Numbly, I walked into the house, where my mother stood at the kitchen sink.

"Where is Fido?"

"Sit down, son, we need to talk."

"I don't want to talk, I just want to know where she is."

She dried her hands inside of a dish towel and shook her head. "We shouldn't have let you get so attached...but it happened so quick...just got out of hand. And now," she tossed a hand toward the shed, "we'd of had to keep it locked up, and it would have probably dug out..." She shook her head again, looked down.

"I went to Doc McCann's place yesterday and he was goin' to let me work out two dollars to get her fixed. Tomorrow, Mom...tomorrow."

"Your father came and got it at noon." The words were spoken in monotone, not coldly, and she quickly spun and walked away.

I climbed the stairs to my room and sat on the edge of the bed, finally flopping backward, where I remained for two hours. I did not shed a single tear. I simply wiped my soul clean of dogs, all the while wondering how long it would be before the glowing blade of hatred cooled. I got up when I heard the rumble and down shift of my father's truck as it turned into the drive. From the window I watched as he emerged—a slow motion unfolding of limbs—from the cab, the little bolt action single-shot .22 caliber rifle in his right hand. His shirt was stained dark with grimy sweat, his back bowed as if the shirt weighed a hundred pounds. He lifted his feet just enough to scoot his boots through the grass. He did not look up at me, but he knew that I watched. From that day forward, not a word was ever spoken about Fido by me or him or my mother. He lived for another fifty-one years.

I was more fortunate than my father; for thirteen years I was a child, and for two months I loved a dog.

I have a good friend who was a city policeman in 1977. One night, his boredom was wiped away when a call from the dispatcher crackled into his ears, and in the end, he met a man who bore a much greater resemblance to something from the lower regions rather than the plane of earth. The first part of the story is factual, but the ending is fictional. But just barely, according to my friend, who is no longer a cop.

DANCING WITH DEMONS

He must have danced around the edge of the demon fire many times before that night, must have listened to the scratchy voices, seen the images, wondered what it would be like to see her naked body, to feel her writhe beneath his power. When he crossed over the edge of the fire with the knife in his right hand, he must have heard her plaintive whimpers, smelled her—perfume and sweet, female sweat and fear—his brain chocked full of carnal knowledge. But the knife wasn't just a tool for obtaining raw sex. The creatures in the fire whispered and cackled for blood as well, gave the man a peek inside the great slash that would start under her right ear and end under the left, exposing the dangling, wormy ends of vessels and twitching muscle fibers and white, gristly structures as he dug deeper and deeper. He must have been secure with the foreknowledge granted inside the demon fire, counted on it as a done deal.

It began for me at 2:26 am, driving back to the station to write reports. Ninety-nine percent of the city was asleep, but a part of the one percent ramped up my heart rate as the radio crackled with the voice of the dispatcher.

"Burglary in progress, 3700 W. Stewart Road. Any unit."

"Responding, Code 2 from Providence and Cherry."

The big engine roared as the light bar strobed the street, the dispatcher's voice in my car again: "Resident is at home and reports hearing someone trying to get in downstairs."

Adrenaline is a phenomenon that can creep up on cat's paws and slam into the center of your chest, or it can fill your chest incrementally, a dispatcher's sentence at a time. "Intruder is now inside the residence with the occupant." An increment.

Right boot on the accelerator, left boot covering the brake, the sound of tires biting the pavement as I turned west on Stewart Road. The final increment, the voice still cool, dispassionate: "Shots fired."

I screeched to a halt just in front of a second police cruiser. The officer leaped from the car and ran toward me a few steps before we instinctively headed—guns and flashlights drawn—in opposite directions around the little two-story house. A faint rectangle of light seeped through a second-story window blind. The front door was locked, and I waited until my partner rounded the corner of the house and signaled for me to follow him. The back door stood open a few inches; there was no sign of forcible entry. I motioned to my partner that I would go in first, then sweep left; he would break right. Only the beam of the flashlight guided my steps, lighting up the rifled drawers of a bureau on the far side of a small living room. Silence, thick and eerie, yet with its own sound bouncing back and forth inside my head.

I keyed up again: "Where are they?"

"Upstairs, in the bedroom."

Within seconds, I spotted the first treads of a stairway in the back corner of the room. It was narrow and steep, the kind that leads to an attic—a tactical deathtrap—without cover or possibility of lateral movement. I paused, gathered myself, shouted up the stairs, "Police! Come out with your hands up!" A deafening silence rolled down the stairs. I repeated my command; silence reigned.

"Oh well…into the chute we go…"

I low-crawled up the stairs—flashlight in left hand, gun in right—into the unknown, seeking. The top tread passed from view as I got my first peek into the tiny room. Then I saw him, the man who danced with demons—Caucasian, bear-like, young—standing at the foot of the bed clad only in white briefs. His hands were in the surrender position, the right hand and chest smeared with blood. I trained my sights on him as I inched around the corner, saw a young woman in a thin nightgown sitting on her heels in the middle of her bed. The telephone was on the floor, the receiver lying beside it. Ten feet separated her from the bleeding man. Both of her trembling hands were wrapped around the little .38 snub-nosed revolver, right forefinger on the trigger, hammer cocked. She hadn't seen me. Good. My mind slowed, almost mechanically digesting the situation, sorting options. *When she sees you, she will whirl and so will the cocked gun and the twitchy finger.* I inched backward, a snake in reverse, kept the man in view.

"Police! Keep your hands up!"

The man slowly turned his head toward me, relief leaking through his features. I peered around the corner, confirmed that the girl had not moved—a frozen, trembling statue pointing a gun. I turned off my command voice, said, "I'm a policeman…it's all right now, you can put your gun down."

"No! Lemme see your badge!"

"Okay." I slowly stepped into full view as her eyes darted at me, registered the uniform. "Don't point your gun at me, please…just him…not me."

She locked back on the man, again totally focused, white-knuckling the gun, finger on the trigger. I spoke softly, urgently. "Lay the gun down now."

"No."

"All right then, how about if I move over there and get it? My gun…and my partner behind me…both of us are going to keep our guns on him. How about it?"

Her head bobbed slightly. "O…o…okay."

I walked to the bed, then carefully slipped the web of my free hand between the cocked hammer and the frame of the revolver, slipped it from her fingers, uncocked it and shoved it into my back pocket. For the first time, I heard the sounds of breathing in the close air of the room. I moved quickly to the wounded man, saw that his trousers were down around his ankles. On the floor beside the wad of trousers was the knife—five inch blade with a wooden handle. As my partner cuffed him, I looked closer at his hand and chest. There was an entry wound on the outside of his right hand, and the missing thumb tip marked the bullet's exit path. There was no wound to his chest, the bloody streak the result of the hand wound. She had fired only one shot.

Dispatch called, and I answered, "One in custody, stable, minor wound, but send an ambulance."

My partner pulled the man's trousers up, zipped and buckled them, and then hustled him from the room. I turned toward the girl. She was still drawn into a bundle on her bed, now wrapped in a terrycloth nightgown.

"It's over," I said, "it'll help if you make yourself take a couple of really deep breaths."

She nodded, made an attempt. "This is a nightmare."

"Was...not 'is.'" I paused, said. "I'm Tim. What's your name?"

"Janet."

"Are you a student?"

"Yeah. University...first-year med school."

"Can you take me through it now?"

She nodded again, poked her tongue through her lips for a second. "You've heard about the bump in the night thing. That's exactly what I heard. I hadn't been asleep long, and then I was awake...and the sound was already gone sort of... but it wasn't really...God, that doesn't make sense, but..."

"It makes perfect sense, Janet."

"Anyway, I kinda doubted the sound, and it went back to real quiet...and like a dummy, I started down the stairs, got halfway, and then I knew he was in the house...I mean footsteps..." She stopped, shook her head. "I'm pretty sure I peed on myself then, and I whirled around and ran back up, but he was so quick...I mean, I couldn't believe how fast he was...and when I turned around all I saw was the knife."

She looked at me, finally drew a decent breath, as if she was beginning to focus on the sweet "now" of her extended life. "He asked me where the money was, and I told him I only had a few dollars, and that pissed him off...but it was never about the money...and he said, 'if there's no money, I'll just take something better.' The bastard...the lousy-ass bastard, he pulls out a roll of tape...and I knew that if he ever got that on me I might be as good as dead...you know."

She was rocking to and fro, a steady rhythm, looking straight ahead at the wall, reeling it all back in for me. "The gun was in my purse, on the floor beside the bed...I can't believe he didn't see my purse, and grab it...God, how did he miss it?...and then..." She stopped rocking, shook her head, looked at me. "You believe in God?"

"Sometimes, I think."

"Yeah...I'm like that too."

I waited. She began to rock again, the same rhythm, as precise as a pendulum. She looked back at the wall. "I swear I have no idea where the words came from...I was scared out of my mind...and then...I rubbed my hands over my boobs, and calm as can be, I said, 'Hey, you're the boss, but if you don't tape me up, we can both enjoy it.' He liked that. He didn't put the knife down, and he unbuckles and unzips, and I waited for his pants to go down...knew it had to be then. I rolled over and got the gun before he realized what was happening."

"Young lady, that was a bit of genius."

She shook her head, sat still in the bed now, looked more like twelve than twenty. "I think it was a miracle."

"Who can say...could've been."

"Then the bastard says, 'You think you can stop me with that toy gun?' 'It's no toy,' I said. 'You fuckin' bitch,' he says, and he shook one leg loose from his pants and started for me...and...I don't even remember the sound. Can you believe that? I swear, I don't remember the sound...just the blood splattering and the smoke...and he looked really surprised, and...well...you know the rest."

With the same dainty forefinger that pulled the trigger, she reached up and coaxed a sweaty curl of brown hair across her brow. "Am I in trouble? I mean...Daddy wasn't really sure about me having it in my purse, especially when I'm outside, and Momma threw a fit...but in the end, he won out. He said I was going to the city, alone."

"No, you're not in any trouble. Don't worry about that."

The tears finally came and I could see the weariness descend on her, push her shoulders down. The ambulance siren yelped, a block away. "I want to talk to Daddy now."

"Sure, call him now. Take as long as you want, then get dressed for me and we'll go to the station and we can formalize your statement. My partner will wait for you downstairs."

"Where will you be?"

"I need to take an ambulance ride with the guy."

"The lousy-ass bastard."

From the damsel to the demon—hell of a gear shift—but that's what cops do a lot. And I got this shift right. Dead bang. You'll see what I mean later. If I would have done the Miranda drill, jumped in by the book, he would have clammed up, denied my look inside the demon fire. I uncuffed him, waited until the EMT taped some gauze over his thumb. I told the EMT to ride up front, and that I'd ride in back with the suspect. He nodded, said, "All right, I guess. Let me get him sorted out for the ride. Rules and all, you know."

"Got it, sure."

I studied the young man as the tech got him situated on the gurney and locked the wheels into place. Handsome, dark hair, well trimmed, maybe twenty-five, could have been a tight end, or just a workout freak. When the tech started to strap him in, the man raised his uninjured hand and knocked the strap out of the tech's hand.

The tech stood, said, "Whatever, dude…this buggy hits the ditch and my story is that you unstrapped your own ass."

"Cool by me. Just leave me the hell alone."

The tech shot me a glance before he hopped out the back and slammed the doors. I plopped down on the bench seat on the other side of the compartment.

I pulled my hat off, let it rotate in my fingertips, then puffed out a breath of air loud enough for him to hear. "Man, you had a near-death experience up there, huh?"

"Fuck you, wise guy. I ain't sayin' shit till my old man gets a lawyer."

"Easy there, okay. I know the drill. We climb out of this vehicle and let it play out however it goes…no hard feelings on my part. It's like this conversation never happened."

"So why bother? You want to amuse yourself, why don't you whip out your dick and play with that."

The first lie slid off my tongue like warm water. "Hey, I'm just glad your hand got in the way. I'd hate to see a guy shot dead over a simple piece of ass."

I flipped my hat around, looked down, but I saw his head rotate a fraction, felt his eyes for a second. "I'll bet."

"I'm not shitting you. I've been around the block… haven't been a cop forever, and won't be one forever." I crept forward into his world, felt the heat rise as the ring of fire crept closer. "You think I didn't see those nice stand-up titties nosing through the nightgown? Get real. What is a curiosity though is why a stud like you needs a knife. Bet you've sacked up with your share in a college town like this."

"Lost count."

"I don't doubt that, man. I didn't do too bad myself."

The drive train droned loud underneath us, filled the compartment. I waited for a few seconds, then said, "Just a curiosity…the knife, you know."

"You know, mister policeman, I honestly can't figure out if you're fuckin' with me or not, but my thumb is starting to throb, and I think I'll amuse myself…since…like you said, this conversation ain't even happening." He looked at me, waited for me to look at him. He smiled. "You probably don't have the balls to ever try to find out for yourself, but there's a sweet difference between gettin' pussy and takin' pussy." He smiled again.

I nodded. "It might be a little risky for my tastes, but I see where you're comin' from."

"You don't see some of where I'm comin' from, mister policeman. You don't see the part where I cut her nice white throat from ear to ear." He rolled his head, looked straight up. "Now you're wondering if I'm fuckin' with you, right?" He huffed a dry laugh. "Gurgle, gurgle, and hiss, hiss goes her windpipe. How you like those sounds, mister policeman? I don't think it's over between me and that little bitch back there." He raised his bandaged hand. "Think I'll make her suck on this stub for a while before we get down to the good stuff. That'd be just about perfect, huh?"

It was then that I began to hear sounds ricochet around inside my head—discordant music, but not unpleasant, just damn strange—and my heart ramped up as the volume rose. I wasn't even sure that I wanted to chase it away, but I did partly, only because the demon man began to talk again, and I wanted to hear him, had to hear him.

"Yep, gonna do the little bitch one day. Slick-ass lawyer stands up there in front of twelve dumbfucks in the jury box and tells 'em about her little S and M secrets, the steak knife—which came out of her kitchen drawer, mister policeman—was just a prop...and the tape, oh, she liked the tape... like all the times before...and all of a sudden she pulls a gun...and naturally I fear for my life and try to take it from her, then my lawyer gets her so stupid and blabby and her mommy and daddy are watching her, and those twelve people and the judge are staring at her...and...well, you get the picture, huh?"

He rolled his head toward me, smiled, made a sound in his throat like a big cat purring. "Never a day behind bars,

I'm bettin'…parole…some brain-dead jerk in a sixty-nine dollar suit that I'll play like a violin."

I want to believe in Heaven, don't want to believe in Hell. What I heard then came from one place or the other. Up there? Down there? Don't know. Maybe something lurks inside all of us, like a puzzled soldier, waiting for the bugle call. A soldier of the cross or a soldier of the fire? Can't say for sure; I just know that I heard the bugle. Damn, it came quick—the whole layout—scenes unfolding behind my closed eyelids like the old cliché about a man's life flashing before him as he dies. Only it wasn't me that was about to die. It played out like a grainy black and white movie in real time, no dreamy, drawn-out, slow motion bullshit about it. The preview reel stopped with the first gun shot.

I glance to the front of the vehicle to make sure that I see the back of two heads, and then turn slightly from the demon man so that my gun side is shielded. With my right hand, I draw the nine-millimeter pistol smoothly, leave the thumb safety engaged. I throw my body on top of his, left hand clutching a handful of black hair, my legs wrapping around his, and then we are on the floor. The pistol is pinched between our chests and I'm pulling his hair. Our screams mingle, his real, mine for effect. I make sure he stays on top of me as I shove the muzzle of the gun against my left shoulder, careful to keep the angle shallow. I release the thumb safety and pull the trigger.

The pain is white hot and my screams are as real as his now, but I can only feel them in my throat, my hearing consumed by the gunshot. Five more seconds of soundless screams. I move the muzzle under his chin and pull the trigger and it feels like I'm a child again and another kid has just splashed my face with water from a toy bucket, and for a second I wonder why it feels warm instead of cold. I scream a final time as I shove the weight of the dead aside.

It all went down wonderfully well that night, as did the months that followed. All I ended up with in my file was a reprimand for allowing my suspect to jump me and almost gain control of my weapon. But like I explained, he was one powerful, strapping lad, and highly motivated to boot. Yes, I should have paid more attention to the strange stuff he was spouting just before his attack, but all cops hear the like from time to time. The EMT testified about how aggressive he was resisting the safety straps. But his father was a ten-ured professor at the university, very well connected, and he began to wail to the press. But then came my lie-detector test, which I passed with flying colors. After that, my internal guys were really charged up and did some nice work—turned up two other girls willing to testify regarding his "violent" and "threatening" sexual proclivities. Funny how tongues tend to loosen after the perp who did the threatening gets chunked in the clay. Don't ask me how I passed the lie-detector, I don't know. I could have been talking to a sweet little lady on a park bench about the way the clouds looked, or how old the Pekinese in her lap was. Calm from hell? Or from heaven? You decide.

It's been twelve years now, and I still can't decide. Thing is, I don't even care anymore. What I do care about is that Janet is alive. Our lives came together on the night of the demon fire like two balls ricocheting inside a pinball machine, but I've followed her career from a distance. Pediatric oncology, practices in the Kansas City metro area. Shepherds little kids and their parents down the long, shadowy tunnel called can-cer. Word is that she's damn near a saint. About a year ago, I saw a photo of her in a local paper along with a nice write-up.

She was sitting on a bench with four kids—two boys and two girls. At least I think so. Hard to tell when they're so young and completely bald. I must have stared at the photo for two minutes before it struck me that nobody was looking at the camera. She had the kids gathered in her arms and they were all looking up at her face, and she was looking down at the smallest kid, maybe three years old. It reminded me of a picture I saw once—seems like about a hundred years ago—of Jesus surrounded by several little children and a couple of lambs. It moved me. You've probably seen one like it too. So help me, I got the same feeling when I saw Janet in that photo. Only difference was that Jesus' kids had hair. Maybe her job is harder than his. Or maybe Jesus is in the photo with her and the dying kids. That's what she said in the article, in so many words. Reckon it's just me that can't see him. She's the saint.

Me? I know I'm not saint material. I stayed on the force for three years after that night, but I never really trusted myself. It wasn't that I ever felt guilt—and I mean ever. What drove me away was the possibility that I might meet another man who danced around the edge the demon fire, and the same strange sounds would crank up in my head along with that black and white preview reel, but this time it would turn out to be a campfire—guys sitting around listening to metal rock, laughing uproariously, farting, drinking beer—not a damn demon in sight. Joke's on me. But I've already whacked some poor bastard who got up to dance to Led Zep, which would mean that the sounds in my head came from hell.

Like I said, I can't decide where they came from, and don't think I care. Or maybe in a core-deep chamber of my soul that won't tolerate a lie, I do care, and just don't ever want to know the truth. Because maybe the truth is that the dead man was really no more than a young, mouthy shitbag full of wind—a farter at a campfire—just amusing himself with a mouthy shitbag of a cop. Maybe his professor daddy would have gotten him sorted out, and he would have found Jesus, and studied medicine, cured cancer. Goddamn. I've got to stop.

I do hope that Janet lives for a hundred years.

I do hope I don't.

You?

This is an essay from Heaven, or Hell, or both. I am unable to decide.

OF STRAW-HAIRED GIRLS AND STILLED ANGELS

Now I lay me down to sleep, I pray the Lord my soul to keep

She had a gap-toothed smile under a button nose, and over these were wide-set green eyes, and reaching down to the eyes were wispy bangs the color of sunlit straw, and her voice squeaked melodies that tumbled words when she was happy. Then they came—her step father and his friend. Asleep, her fuzzy shoes with floppy bunny ears beneath the bed, dreaming of frilly, pink blouses and girl friends' chatter, and the look of the white frosting on her birthday cake— this was the child slithered to in darkness. A seeker of bodies found her broken one stuffed into a crack inside a cave, deep in the woods not far from her home. The inspector of bodies revealed that she was repeatedly violated before her life was extinguished with a cord looped around her dainty neck— a form of execution recently made notable by dog-fighters exposed for culling their stock with a flair for torture. And now the church folk of the little town in southwest Missouri will weep and mourn, will again drop to their knees and pray as fervently as they had on hopeful days before the seeker completed his work. Flowers, both fresh and artificial, and teddy bears and notes with hand-drawn hearts, and photographs will soon form colorful layers on the cold ground of winter encircling her tombstone, and in the spring they will be wilted and faded and tattered and some will have been loosed by Eolian fingers and cast into fields beyond the cemetery. But some of the parting gifts will survive, perhaps as long as she did, which is a very long lifespan for the things the mourners left her, but a pitiful lifespan for the little girl herself. She was nine years old, a terminal age.

I proceed from shaky ground. Some say that angels attend all children, from birth to that vague point in later life when they are released from duty. Surely, they must be a sad troop in general, although frenziedly active, requiring frequent exhortations from Michael or Gabriel, say, every few seconds, given routine earthly proceedings. I believe in the existence of angels, and to rage at them must be tantamount to raging at God Hisownself, or perhaps worse, if one believes—as I do—that angels are lesser beings than man, thus unable to fend off the arrows shot by man that I doubt pierce the Creator to the point of anguish. The author of Hebrews tells us: "For indeed He does not give aid to angels, but He does give aid to the seed of Abraham." Most theologians would claim that this is out of context, thus accusing me of cheating here, given their insistence that the author is referring specifically to the second chance at salvation afforded mankind, while fallen angels are irreversibly doomed. In or out of context, the passage leads me to believe that man ranks higher on the holy totem pole than angels. Further, the dispensation of divine aid—whether sweeping or particular—seems perfectly backward to me, exasperating actually, especially when applied to this singular, monstrous category of sin by man, and witnessed by stilled angels.

Picking on angels can't be spiritually healthy; nevertheless, I proceed. Where was the straw-haired girl's hovering angel? On celestial break? Were his eyes wandering elsewhere, like an indolent sentry lulled into complacence by yet another quotidian nightfall, sure to be a replica of the one just passed? Or was his attention where it should have been, on his tiny charge, so helpless under her blanket, so vulnerable to the predators? This seems to me the plausible scenario; I can't get the image of an incompetent angel to take shape anywhere in my brain. Thus, the mighty warrior's hand was stilled, and he watched (with horror, or stoicism, or both, or neither?) as the blanket was ripped from her body and the teddy bear that she couldn't yet give up tumbled to the floor. He watched, as cruel fingers gouged at virginal flesh, and when bruised open, watched as adult organs penetrated again and again, rending asunder. And he listened too, did the stilled angel, as she shrieked in her agony, and finally, when they had their fill, as the shrieks subsided into gurgles as the cord drew tighter and her bowels voided and Death arrived on the lowly, vulgar scene.

Years ago, I posed this question about the stilled angels of brutalized children to a deeply Christian lady anchored by unshakable beliefs. She attempted to assure me that no matter the gruesome circumstances of a child's demise, the attendance of the hovering angel was a certainty. At the time, I was merely miffed by the stilling (my rage evidently requiring dozens more slaughtered children to achieve crescendo), so I didn't reveal my gnawing doubts. I wanted to ask her if she thought the angel somehow rendered the child to a state similar to that of a stunned impala as it loses various body parts to a casually munching pride of lions. Or if the angel just hung around until the twitching ceased, his only duty being the whisking away of the newly departed soul. But I asked neither question then. Now I do, to myself, and I have no answers, only suspicions. The rage persists. Tomorrow it will have diminished a bit, and next week even more, but in a month or two, when the next child's photo stares at me first from the newspaper, then from a crack in the rocks, or a shallow grave, it will boil up again. I fear that it will be stronger.

No, it is not this fettered angel at whom I rage, it is God. Why? With all my being, I believe that the soul of the straw-haired girl is safe, and will one day be joined again with her precious body—whole, pure, undefiled—and that a hundred years from now, much less a million, the manner of her death will be of cosmic unimportance. Yet I rage, and it feels so absolutely justified now, with her body barely cold in the ground under all of those delicate remembrances, and with her killers guaranteed nutritious meals, climate-controlled shelter, medical care, suitable recreation, and legal defenders who will dredge up all manner of technical absurdities in a herculean effort at preventing the only justice that makes sense to me. I know very well what I am instructed to feel and say; I know very well of the Biblical ratiocination that should ratchet through my brain and prop me up and wipe away her smiling photo and cause me to proclaim aloud, "All things work together for good to those who love God," and the rest of that Pauline wisdom that resounds from funeral homes and church sanctuaries and living rooms of weathered houses in the Ozarks of Missouri. And yet I rage. I should be very careful here, but I resent the self-admonishment despite its source. "Vengeance is mine, saith the Lord." Yes, I know, I know, but goddamn the killers. Now. Please. I bond with the vocal vulture in the classic cartoon. The feathered thinker is perched on a limb with a silent partner as they peer down at tasty rabbits and squirrels scampering about, and he says, "The hell with this waiting, I'm gonna kill something." So it is with the two murderers of the straw-haired girl. The hell with the waiting; I see no point in it.

I once was among the flock of a pastor who, several years ago, attended an inmate named Ralph down in the dead-man-walking sector of the Potosi Correctional Facility. Ralph was about to receive the ultimate correctional attention. Only a few years prior to the fateful night, Ralph was welcomed with open arms by the pastor as a new convert to Christianity, and this largely due to the leading of Ralph's wife, Susan. I remember her quite well, having sat beside her during many Sunday School sessions. She was a sweet lady, delightfully talkative, and insightful on occasion. I liked her. After his trip down the sanctuary aisle to embrace the pastor, Ralph—to the utter amazement of all witnesses, chief among the amazed being the pastor—snatched the microphone from his hand and loosed a decent five-minute rendition of a televangelist in full sweat. After that, Ralph joined his wife for a few Sunday mornings before disappearing from Sunday School class, and then Susan disappeared from class, then from earth altogether. The facts crystallized when dogged police investigators forced open the storage unit within which Ralph had hidden her car. Blood splatters and bone fragments told a story of death by shotgun—albeit a decent way to perish compared to strangulation following violation. The pastor viewed the final drama in the death chamber as the poison flooded Ralph's veins and he coughed and quivered his way past life's thin veil. Post-Potosi, and after zealous reflection on the overwhelming scene, the pastor proclaimed to all who would listen (many likely preferring not to, with one listener assuredly in this category) that he was no longer certain of the validity of the death sentence, and that he doubted that the body Missouri had accomplished anything remotely resembling righteous retribution by banishing Ralph from the land of the living. Personally, I hope the technician low-dosed the poison drug vials, thus causing the sorry bastard great pain, this hope running tandem with another greater hope that he had ample time to remember the look in Susan's eyes as she faced the shotgun. I know in my heart of hearts—without a scintilla of doubt—that I could push the big, red poison chemical buttons, or pull the trigger of a rifle, or release the trap door on the scaffold, or, preferably, tie the straw-haired girl's killers to a tree in my woods and go to carving. I think that I would urge them to accept Jesus before the carving got too deep, although clouds of uncertainty rapidly thicken here. With or without an explanation of the saving grace of Jesus, I would indeed finish my task.

I nearly talked myself into making a visit to the child's grave. I envisioned myself standing there in front of her tombstone, hands folded respectfully, head bowed, prayerful even, as I sought solace in the nearness of her physical remains. But that scene quickly faded, replaced with another photograph from the other side of death that was recently burned onto the inside of my eyelids. It was in a *National Geographic* magazine featuring the catacombs of Palermo, Sicily, and the arresting skillfulness of an embalmer far ahead of his time. Ensconced within a tiny glass-covered casket was the body of a little girl with straw-colored bangs who had succumbed to pneumonia in 1920, yet appearing to me as if living flesh and blood in the midst of a peaceful slumber, soon to rise and resume a vibrant life, so perfect was the artistry. Without doubt, her family and young friends wept and mourned on the occasion of her death, yet the manner of her passing was I think, if not acceptable in the truest sense of the term, still bearable, given the absence of marks of savagery. Should I ever stand over the straw-haired girl's casket, I am certain that ghastly visions of her death wounds would issue from the grave and stoke my rage even more, despite the means available to her modern day embalmer.

The only trip that tempts is one to Potosi Correctional Center, where one of her killers resides. I could cobble together some sort of lie—a sympathetic Ted Bundy-style interview perhaps, seeking to tell his poor story of a life ruined by bad choices—and over time, gain the trust of the killer and his keepers. And then, when they least expect it, spring like Hannibal Lecter in a movie, chomping away like a hungry fiend before being clubbed off of my prey. I am a strong man, and it is possible that I could connect with the jugular vein, thus having the pleasure of carrying out the death sentence while inflicting great pain and spillage of blood. Yet I know that I will never visit the killer; I am too cowardly to take his place at Potosi. He will remain in his prison; I will remain in mine.

Having so precisely positioned myself on the lower plane, I wonder just where I will be on the higher—beyond the phantom wall that separates the planes. There are peculiar chambers in my mind, and I fear their contents. Yet I have cracked open their doors, peeked inside, spilled here some of what I saw. No doubt, my Christian friend who defends attending angels (and by extension, God—though she would make no such outlandish claim) would tell me that the chambers are Satan's creations, allowed to form by spiritual slippage. She might even tell me—assuredly, out of love—that I should get my soul sorted out, lest I risk joining the fallen angels in their plunge into eternal darkness. Very possible, that, but the chambers damn sure feel like my very own creations, and I don't fear them enough to pray for their closing. I wonder if that lack of fear constitutes outright apostasy, or if it is the manifestation of a backslidden fool—still salvageable— dancing madly at the edge of a demon fire, or if indeed there is any difference between those pitiful conditions in the eyes of the Great Judge. Clearly, I'm diminished here, made less by my rage as I perch on the limb with the two vultures, nodding vigorous affirmation for the impatient speaker's plan, bewildered by the silence of his partner. Even if I do pass final muster, will I be lessened in eternity, moved many streets (or miles, or realms, or whatever unit is deemed appropriate by measuring authorities) away from First Street in Paradise City, Eternity—no zip code necessary—thus downgraded by my blasphemy? Surely it is so. May God forgive me; I'm all right with that.

If I should die before I wake, I pray the Lord my soul to take.

If only the straw-haired girl had died before she waked. If only. It all would have played out so much easier for the both of us, and for the attending angel, who continues his flights to lowly earth.

In stillness.

This story is taken from a Civil War novel entitled *Chimborazo,* which I wrote many years ago. A strong female character emerged within the confines of a mail car of a Confederate train.

NELDA CRUMP

The woman awoke from her uneasy slumber, the metallic clack of the door bolt sharp in her ears. It was the first time that the man had locked the door to the mailroom. She blinked against the weariness, felt the return of the ponderous rhythm of the train as it rolled northeastward. She had ridden one train or another for four days now and there were still three long hours remaining. She focused on the expansive, roseate face of the mail agent, saw an ugliness deeper than his visage, saw it in the thick-lipped grin: an unwelcome wordless message. The delicate but comforting weight of the derringer pistol in her dress pocket rested atop her right thigh. Tied to the same leg, just below her knee, was a bone-handled knife with a six-inch blade in a leather sheath. She had honed the blade to a razor's edge the night before departing her little homestead five miles south of Huntsville, Alabama.

The woman and the man had shared the small room since early morning, when the mail agent had prevailed on the colonel in command of the train, insisting that arrangements could be made. The Danville depot was congested with soldiers, and the boarding troops had caused the colonel to order from the train the few remaining civilians. The woman had forcefully argued her case, explained that she was on an errand of mercy, but to no avail until the agent interceded. She had given him her heartfelt thanks, promised not to be a bother.

Her clothing was homespun and functional, dark in color, and did not attract attention. Like a soft brown rope, a thick braid of hair trailed down her back. Her features were pleasant, thought not striking, the lines of her trim body hidden by the dress, as she had intended. Her hands were coarse and broad across the knuckles, and she moved her right hand now to the top of the pocket. The agent looked at her again, a second too long, and she nodded curtly at him as he lumbered toward her.

"Well, how are we a doin' now, little missssyyy?"

She was certain now, the whiskey slur a clear portent. The weariness was gone; she shifted her position slightly, planted both shoes firmly on the floor, said, "Just fine, thanks."

"Ahhh...that's good...good." He pulled a small flask from his coat pocket. "Bit nippy in here, don't you think? This here ain't the best I ever tasted but it lights a little fire inside." He chuckled thickly, his shoulders bouncing up and down with the sounds. "Have a little nip with me, won't you now?"

"Don't care for any. Thanks just the same."

His mouth straightened into a firm line, then downward at the corners. "For a gal who's been done a mighty big favor, you ain't a'tal sociable."

"I thanked you proper...and I meant it. We've talked some, you've done your mail sortin'...I've done my ridin'. The trip is about over now."

He took two gulps from the flask. "Not for three hours or so, it ain't." He pocketed the flask, reached behind him and dragged his chair forward. He plopped down with a long sigh, his knees within a foot of her dress.

The woman locked her gaze with his, moved her hand slowly into the dress pocket, said, "Surely we can stay mannerly toward each other for three more hours."

The tip of his tongue darted from the corner of his mouth, swept slowly between his lips. "I'se hopin' that you had sense enough to see that I'm tryin' to be reeeel mannerly, missy. Your soldier man's been gone a long time, ain't he?" He raised the forefinger of his right hand like a child about to dip it into the frosting of a cake, and then extended it across the space between them, touched the tip to her knee. "Way I see it...you can stop feelin' lonely right now here with me...all cozy in our little room. Sort of a warm up for your man, don't you see?"

"Move your finger back, mister."

He spread his fingers, clamped them over her knee. She could see the sweat beads glistening from the fleshy cavities below his eyes, feel the fingers begin to creep above her knee. In a blur of movement, she drew the derringer from her pocket and aimed it squarely at the bridge of his nose. The hammer cocked with a firm snick, the gun steady in her hand.

"Welllll...fiesty'un, ain't you now." He slid his fingers from her knee. "Trouble for you is that ain't much of a pistol."

"It might not kill you...true enough. But it'll hurt you long enough for me to pull my knife, and then, mister mail agent, I will gut you like the hog you're actin' like and watch your insides dribble over your boots."

He looked at the small black hole, the steadfast hand, the flinty eyes. Slowly, he straightened his back and with a great wheezing breath, stood, backed away from her. "This here is Confederate gov'ment property. If I'se to go get the colonel and tell him you had a gun in here, he'd throw your sorry ass off this train. Might even lock you up."

"Go ahead and take your stinkin' whisky breath and blow it all over your colonel and see if he comes to check on me. And even if he does, this little pistol will be in a place where a gentleman officer would never look, and then after he leaves, it'll be back in my hand before you can get near me."

The agent snorted through his nose, narrowed his eyes for a moment as he shook his head as if to clear it of some implausible vision. He dragged the chair back to his desk, sank into it, the passion suddenly and strangely nothing more than a cloudy memory. He looked at her now, held up a meaty paw, waved it like a flag of surrender. "Put the pistol up, will you…some of them triggers are a mite flinchy."

She pointed the derringer at the ceiling, eased the hammer down, slid the weapon into her pocket. "Do we have an understandin' then?"

"We do."

He turned away from her, began to poke at the pieces of mail strewn over his desk. The great rattle and hum of the rails filled the room, calmed the raw nerves of both the man and the woman. The agent glanced at her first, was relieved to see both of her hands empty in her lap, then he looked at her face.

"The whiskey…it…uh…sometimes clouds my thinkin' a little." He mouthed a raspy little laugh at himself.

"I'd say a sight more than a little. It right near cost you your life."

"Anyways…no hard feelin's, huh?"

"I'd as soon put it behind us."

Another puff of air pushed through his lips as he raised his hand, flopped it down on the desk. "Where'd you say he was...your man?"

"Hospital in Richmond. Place called Chimborazo."

"Leg, you say?"

"Right leg. Cannon ball to the knee at a place called Boydton Plank Road, then knife and saw to the high thigh in the hospital."

He looked down at his desktop, did not see the envelopes. "No offense intended, but...you're a country gal, ain't you?"

She stared at him for a long moment, read his mind. She nodded once, said, "Yes, we country gals can survive."

"Never did catch your name."

"Never said it."

"I'd like to know it."

"Nelda...Nelda Crump."

The man made a sound in his chest, low and fervent. "He's a mighty lucky man."

She locked on his eyes, dared him to look away, but he did not. "He'd be a better man than I am a woman even if the blue bastards would've shot everything away but his heart."

"Ummmm...I'd take issue with that...bet he would too."

Suddenly weary again, Nelda looked down at her hands, thoughts of the grueling return journey with her broken man filling her brain like stones collecting in a sack. "It'll take all the heart both of us have left to get him home."

"Goddamn, but I do hope y'all make it."

She nodded, filled her lungs with the stuffy air, said, "Oh, we'll make it, Mister Mailman...we will make it home to Alabam'.

I have a high school classmate (Class of 1966) who lives alone near the Missouri River. At heart, he once was just a farm boy. But then he went halfway around the world and saw and did more than he could deal with. And now his heart is lost, and I'm not certain that he will ever again find it.

TRAINS BY THE RIVER

Why did Hamlet trouble about ghosts after death, when life itself is haunted by ghosts so much more terrible?

Chekhov, *Notebooks,* **1892-1904**

He sits in a green vinyl recliner patched with duct tape in a paint-peeled house one hundred yards from a steep cliff that descends to the Missouri River, and on cold mornings in early spring, when the fog is high and smoky above the water, he says that he can't claim for absolute goddamn sure that Vietnam isn't on the other side, a gaggle of Montagnards flaying alive a staked Vietcong who spits at them and makes not a sound as they paint their faces with knives coated in his blood and feed his skin like limp parchment to snarling dogs.

"I'm not sure any of the little fuckers were even half human, either bunch of 'em. Especially the Yards, even though they were on our side. They had this sacrifice ritual, did it every year or so, they'd tie up a water buffalo and beat it to death with sticks and rocks. Nothing else allowed. Just like their ancestors did it a thousand years ago. I watched it once…for a while anyhow. Never felt so sorry for a critter in my life. It takes a while to put down a big old buff with sticks and rocks. A helluva while." He pauses, the fingers of his right hand extended, as if electrified for a second. "They were tougher than us, the Vietnamese and the Yards both. I'm sure of that. They're still there, still trying to murder each other. Me, I've been through a half dozen VA shrinks, had my wife finally leave me after thirty years, and until about a month ago, didn't know whether to read my Bible or tear it into a thousand pieces right before I took a flyin' leap off yonder cliff."

He smiles, thin and mirthless, through a long, grey beard that looks like it might be hiding a family of mice. I haven't seen or heard from him since high school graduation night, not once. The phone call came out of the blue. Save for his eyes, the beard hides his visage, but I still see James, long face, easy smile—crooked and infectious—one front tooth lapped slightly over the other. I see him in his blue corduroy Future Farmers of America jacket, the hand-sized FFA lettering gold on his back. I think I remember that he won a blue ribbon once for a heifer at the Moniteau County Fair, but I can't say for sure. His speech pattern is exactly the same, like a man in a contest to see who can talk the slowest. The smile fades. "My luck, probably snag my ass halfway down on a tree limb and take a week to give up the ghost. Joke's on me, huh? Damn joke's lasted about forty-two years now, my sorry ass snagged on that limb." He looks up at me. "I ain't asking for pity, you understand. I don't pity myself. It's like…wonderment or some such…like a long strange fucken dream that ought to be over, but I'm still in it." He shakes his head. "I don't expect you to understand. I don't even care if you do." He pauses, looks out the window. "But I called you, huh? Why the hell did I do that if I don't care that you don't care?"

"I do care." He nods his head and I think he means to thank me.

"Then there came this other dream I got to tell you about after a while. But there's other stuff first. There was this light colonel, a real ladder-climber, gonna be a general officer at a very young age, don't you know. Long on speeches to his hero troops who were going to wipe out every slant-eyed, yellow-skinned gook in Nam and Cambodia both. He never missed a chance to send a platoon or a company out into the shit, sometimes…hell, most times…just to see if we could make contact. Didn't matter a fuck to him if we ran into a battalion or a regiment, hoped we did. Then he'd get in a chopper and swoop around the sky, watching the proceedings, like a football coach in the air, urging his boys to kick ass, stop 'em, then make a touchdown so he could chalk up another win. The guy that shot him down with an M-60 was a big old farm boy named Dexter, from Alabama. That night, I asked him if it was a hard shot. 'Oh hell no, he says, 'bout like shootin' at a giant duck. I just led him good, and the belt feedin' one out of five tracers…shit, man, not hard at all. The pilot was open to my side, nothin' 'tween me and him but air. Only real worry was not bringin' the bird down, 'cause I knew damn well they could figure out where it was comin' from. But when I saw him slump over I knew it was a good shoot. Couldn't tell if the colonel got hit too. Hope not. Hope the fucker screamed all the way down, then roasted for a while after the crash.'"

James looked up at the ceiling, at nothing, or something, or everything. "Dexter said that his only regret was having to bring down the pilot too, but it was just one of those tough-shit deals. Him or us, you know. Said he wondered what his momma would think of him if she knew. I told him that if his momma was here and she knew the colonel was using her baby boy's ass for gook bait, she would have got down on all fours and let him prop the 60 over her back for better aim. He said 'yeah, reckon she might've at that.' He let it go after that, we all did, never another single word. The First Sergeant knew what happened, and he was okay with it, totally. The LT might have figured it out, or not, we never knew for sure, but I think he knew we'd of fragged his ass if he squealed. He wouldn't have been the first."

"In the end, what sent me to the shrinks was the chaplain back at the base camp, man of God, don't you know, Major Mallory. Man, he looked the part from head to toe—tall, square-jawed, spit and polish, big black Bible always handy, zipper cover, purple ribbon markers, gold page edges. Cadillac of a Bible. Could preach his ass off. Even had some bad boys from big cities holdin' their hands towards the sky once in a while when he got on a roll about righteous battle and taking down the foe. I thought pretty high of him…until after the Montagnard thing went down."

"We came up on this little ville built into a rocky hillside, and the Yards from the get go were all up in the air about it. Told our interpreter it was filthy with VC sympathizers. The Yards waded in there, yellin' and screamin', but it was all women and kids, a couple old men looked like dried prunes. Before it was over, a lot of butchering took place. We mostly stood back, most of us took a walk and smoked, but I couldn't, like some mindless moth drawn to that flame you read about. I might have got through it if it hadn't been for a little girl, maybe twelve, thirteen…beautiful face, raven hair, great big ole black eyes. There was this one Yard, we called him The Crab. About the size of a hundred and twenty-five-pound chimp, and damn near as strong. Had hands like a man twice his size, and these nails, thick as clam shells and long, woulda done for a damn werewolf under a full moon. He wore a necklace of dried ears, but not a one was cut off. He just ripped 'em off. I saw him do it a couple times. Unbelievable…like you would tear off the corner of a magazine page. One of our guys claimed that he took the ears so easy because he started at the top with a thumbnail cut."

James falls silent, a man gone to stone, breathless, lifeless, and then it passes with the rise and fall of his chest. I knew what he was going to say.

"The Crab had her by one arm and slung her up against a hut and then he ripped off both of her ears at the same time and just left her there. She didn't scream, she just whimpered, kinda like a pup that had lost its momma, held her hands where her ears used to be. Just whimpered. I'll always regret that I didn't just yell at the Crab and run up to him and put a round through his head before he took her ears, and just live with the consequences. To tell you the truth, if I had, I don't think we'd be having this conversation. I might have turned out halfway normal. But I didn't shoot the little ape. Goddamn me, I can still hear her whimper. I heard it for so long that I went to talk to the chaplain the first day we got back to the base, and I told him about the girl and that I couldn't get her out of my head. You know what the sorry bastard told me? He told me that I was a pussy who needed to grow a set of balls and act like a real trooper and that a lot of hard things happened in war and he told me to get my ass back to my platoon. Well, after that, fuck it all was my motto, and that worked for about five years or so I guess and then it didn't work at all. I'd tell myself that the girl is doing okay, that she would wear that long black hair over the ear holes… doin' all right, don't you know. But I'd know better, I always knew better."

"Well, anyhow, that's when the shrink parade started, and it was an on-and-off thing till about a year ago, and when I came home and told the wife that the sumbitch was clearly crazier than I was and that I wasn't ever...I mean fucken *ever*...goin' back, she said that I would go back or she would leave. I didn't and she did. I still have no idea whatsoever what was goin' on in her mind. I mean, I was never better after a session, not once, and she could surely see that, but somehow, she had it in her mind that my bein' hooked up with these...these...white coats...these professional head docs was my only chance."

He shook his shaggy head and came as close to genuine laughter as I think was possible for him. "Christ smokin' a joint, but they were somethin' I tell you. This one, the last one, he was a peach. Pipe smoker. We'd go out on this little veranda so he could light up. He'd pack and tamp and tamp and pack...great big old bowl carved like the head of an Indian chief...he'd fuck with that thing like it was his last time before climbing the gallows steps, and then he'd finally fire her up and suck that first long drag to the bottom of his lungs and then slow shoot the cloud at my head, like he thought it might hypnotize me I reckon, and he'd look at me through those Coke bottle glasses and say, 'well, James, my friend, let's make some progress today, shall we?' I might say something like, 'Hell yeah, doc, let's do it. Let's play pretend that The Crab regretted his actions toward the little girl and that he found the village medicine man to patch her bloody ear holes and made her feel all better and took her in like a child of his own and that now they loved each other more than life itself and she found a perfect little brown husband and they had beautiful babies that The Crab held in his lap, since he'd become the perfect fucken grandpappy. How's that?' And he'd say something like, 'James, my friend, we've got to get past the bitterness or we'll never find a better place for you.' And I'd say, 'But, doc, the bitterness feels so right, don't you know. Why would we want to make something go away that feels sooooo fucken right, huh? Don't you want me to deal in reality, huh?' That's how it went, but the sumbitch never got rattled, he'd just keep suckin' on that pipe like a Saigon whore on a cock. Then I swear to God, I could see…I mean *see*…his mind wander. It was like watchin' the spokes of a wheel slow down, then just stop." He shook his head as if to clear it. "That last time, he rolls over on one cheek and farts…sounded like somebody rippin' a rotten towel in half…and he says, 'James, my friend, if we could just get you to release your bitterness like I've just released that venomous'…like he was talkin' about a fucken snake for chrissake… 'gas from my system, we'd be so much better off.' We just stared at each other for about five minutes, just stared, while he sucked till his pipe went out."

"Had another one, looked like Walter goddamn Cronkite, I swear. Like to fell over the first time I laid eyes on him, and he said, 'yes indeed, the resemblance is remarkable, isn't it, but we won't let that be a distraction, now will we, James?' He took a particular interest in the chaplain who started this whole mess, kinda like he was more worried that I thought bad of the chaplain than he was that I was leakin' brains faster than a twenty-year-old car leaks oil. Old Cronkite, he tells me that even men of God can become hardened by the things of war and that he was probably suspicious that I was trying to play the crazy card on him, or that he didn't even believe it all went down the way I claimed, and that despite my experience with him, he no doubt brought solace to a great many young soldiers. I told him that the sumbitch absolutely knew for sure what the Yards…and some of us as well…did in lonesome places in the Highlands, and furthermore, it shouldn't make a flyin' fuck to him about anything except using his big old Bible and his high Christian brain pan to help me through my troubles, since that was supposed to be his job, not acting like George Blood and Guts Patton. He never did come back with a decent argument against that. At least he was smart enough to know better than to try that on me.

"Well, anyhow, all that bullshit went on about like that, one form or another. I could tell tales all night about the white coats. I don't think any of 'em really gave a shit to tell you the truth, kinda like us head cases are the same as junk mail to the postman...just job security. But the thing is, I don't really feel hard toward 'em. I mean, really, how can one man get inside the head chambers of another man, when, truth is, he's as fucked up in some way or the other as the man he's supposed to straighten out. I mean, think about it, really. The pipe guy, he's probably thinkin' about screwin' his big-tittied receptionist, or maybe his kid is droppin' acid and he can't stop him. Or maybe, old Cronkite, maybe what he'd really like to do is jump over the desk and strangle my sorry ass and clean up the gene pool a little. Maybe he looks straight at me with those soft eyes and feels his thumbs against my Adams apple. Shit. Get inside another man's head and fix him. Shit. Like taking two balls of snarled binder twine and rubbin' them together and expecting to make a decent square knot. Ain't gonna happen, don't you know."

Dusk falls, weighty and quick, but James makes no move to get up and turn on a light. Minutes pass. A whippoorwill night calls in the distance and then a long freight train rumbles below us on the tracks that border the river. Five minutes long is the train heading into the gathering darkness. He stirs, says, "What is it about a train sound that a man likes so?"

"I can't put my finger on it, but I know what you mean."

"The trains do help me a lot." He huffs a dry laugh. "They help me a thousand times more than the shrinks. Whatcha think they would say about that if they knew?"

"Maybe a real good one would just agree and tell you to live close to the tracks."

He huffs again, louder. "There's none out there that good, I'd bet my nuts in a vise against a Hershey bar. "

"Here's the strange thing, man, or maybe it isn't. I'm finding myself reading my Bible lately. I just read from the New Testament, skip around, the four gospels mainly, maybe a little Paul here and there, but mainly the Jesus stuff, the red letter stuff, don't you know. No Old Testament stuff, too much goddamn bloodshed, I'm full of that already. Does that make sense?"

"Which," I ask, "reading the Bible in general or just the Jesus stuff?"

"I guess it's two questions."

"It makes perfect sense, both ways."

"Strange, I tell you. The urge started creeping up on me not long after the wife left, but it was after the dream about the girl when I knew I had to start. She walks up to Jesus, whimperin' like she always does, her hands over her bloody ear holes, and he's in a white robe, just smiling down at her, and he reaches out with both of his hands and puts them over hers and then pulls them down and her ears are back like The Crab never got hold of 'em. Just like when he put that ear back on the guard that Peter carved on with his sword. I read about that no more'n a day after the dream. I don't think that's a coincidence, myself. Holy Jesus, it was so real, I tell you. I woke up and I'd cried and leaked snot on my pillow."

He is shadowman now, a voice gone silent in the close air of the cluttered living room, but I can feel his energy, the engine of his soul churning in time with the great diesels tugging the freight train now five miles down the tracks. Forearms rise in the owl light as he places his fingers over his ears, strokes their outline. The moon is three-quarter, clean white, and there are no clouds above, and after a time the humble light bleeds through the window panes as if a sentient being, fearful of intrusion. His head slumps forward, chin to chest, like a bone-weary man finally succumbing to sleep, but I know that he is not asleep. He says, "I think I might make it to the proper end, all said and done, but I don't think I want the end to be too far, you understand. Maybe five years, or ten, if I can still keep it together. No more'n that for sure. The five is probably closer to right. That'd be enough. How much more you want?"

"I really haven't thought about it, whatever comes comes."

"That's good, like it ought to be. Only crazies like me calculate years to the grave."

"No, that's not so. Sooner or later, we all calculate, all worry some about hanging around too long."

He raises his head, but otherwise does not stir. "Well, I know you need to get back home, didn't mean to keep you so long."

"It wasn't that long, not long at all. I want you to pick up the phone anytime day or night."

"Oh, I won't be a bother. Last thing I want to be is a bother to anybody." He extends his right hand and I get up, move to his side and take it with both of mine, squeeze firmly. I walk to the front door, ask if he wants a light on. "No, think I'll stay right here for a long while, probably till the midnight freight rolls by. It's a damn fine one, that train, sometimes takes seven or eight minutes. My God, but I hope the trains never stop runnin' down by the river. That might be more'n I could tolerate."

"They won't." I look back a final time. "Stay in the red letters, James." I think I see his head nod, but I'm not certain. He is shadowman again, the inscrutable mass of a spirit, one with the gloaming. Nothing is certain.

Jesus, in His final act of mercy before being nailed to the cross.

Luke 22: 50-51: And one of them smote the servant of the high priest, and cut off his ear. And Jesus answered and said, "Suffer ye thus far." And he touched his ear and healed him.

I don't think that many people ever spend much time look-ing far down the road to old age; they just wake up one day and acknowledge where they are. Sometimes it ends like this. I do not condone, nor do I condemn; either would be very dangerous, and I'm not this old. Yet.

THE TRIP

My Dearest Children,

It was so funny—and we have to have some fun here, or else I won't be able to write this—that last fill up at the Phillips 66. For the last few times, I'd just pull up to the pumps and wait in the car until I saw someone who looked like they might be halfway friendly to an old coot—or coots, if I had your father propped up in the other seat. Anyway, we were both in the car yesterday, and a young man, maybe twenty, glances over and I motion for him to come over. Went like this: Young man, could you see fit to pump our gas for us when you're finished with your own? It won't take much, but we have to have a full tank. Evidently the sight of both of us did the trick. Uh, sure, sure, I can do that he says. He doesn't even go back to his own car. I give him my card and he starts the pump, fills the tank, and brings it back. I thank him profusely, and here's the good part—I love it—I tell him we're going on a looooong trip. He gets kind of a goofy little grin on his face, and can't think of any reply, and I can hear his mind whirring (that is such horse shit (finally I can cuss in front of you), lady, you'll be lucky to make it a block before you run into something) Haaaa!! For goodness sake, don't fret about the trip itself. Just look at how you found us—all curled up together and cozy in the front seat. It just struck me that I wrote that in past tense so I suppose I will go on that way as long as it looks okay. We just turned out the lights at bed time like always but went to the garage and got in the car instead of the bed. We turned the engine on with the heater wide open and rolled down the windows and shut off the headlights so nobody would see light. I am rather proud of thinking of that detail, I must say. And oh yes, Sunday night was no accident since we could tune in the Gospel Hour on AM even if it was a bit staticy (sp?) in the garage. (I am guessing here). There. So much for the trip itself. Well, I should say the <u>beginning</u> of the trip, shouldn't I? I do want to talk about the <u>end</u> of it too, but not now, later.

Oh my, paragraph alert, sorry. I was determined not to get carried away and scrawl out some chunky block, but did it anyway. Remember how I used to harp at the both of you when you would show me your English homework and I could not believe that your teachers let you get away with that? Anyway, everything is organized as far as paper things are concerned. Your father took care of all that long before his mind got weak, and I don't want to waste space carrying on about such things. Besides, it's not like we were Rockerfellers (sp?). Now, about Pastor Fred. I know he will be put out with us, but bless his heart, he won't let on and I know he will come up with decent things to say. I won't try to dictate the service, but if nobody laughs somewhere along the way, we will figure out a way to haunt you both, and the pastor too. Remember the time I got confused trying to put drops in your father's eyes and picked up super glue? He said my God, woman, I can't open my eye and then I looked at that damn little bottle which was the same size as his drops (and don't ask me what they were doing so close) and I said oh sweet Jesus we have to go to the doctor, but it all turned out okay. And here is one on him we never told you about, it embarrassed him so at the time, which was the last time he ever went to the grocery store by himself. I gave him a simple list, maybe 8 or 10 items, and he gets back to the car and starts to put them in and it occurs to him that they aren't sacked, and he told me he said right out loud, oh shit. He looks around the parking lot hoping he doesn't see anybody he knows and pushes the cart back into the store. The checker girl stares at him and says, are you bringing alllll that back for return? And he says, no, honey, I'm bringing it alllll back to paaayy for it! Haaa! I can't believe I kept that a secret until now. I am amazing sometimes. (paragraph alert to the old coot)

Now I know you are wondering just when we (that is not plural by accident, children) decided to do this. It was about 2 months ago around October when the weather started to turn and we started to think about winter. And you know what the wooly worms looked like and my goodness but they were smart little critters. Anyway, back then we began to dread winter, it is so hard on old people. And one day when I had your father on the back deck and he was soaking up the sunshine like a big cat, I thought he was napping as usual, but no. He just up and said over and over, not loud but really from deep down, he said damn damn damn damn and I thought he was having another spell—maybe start in about how a hawk had just plucked him off the ground and dropped him in the hay loft or some such, and the hawk was really Uncle Lester, who he always despised, but his (your father's) father (dead for 30 years) stood below the loft and tried to catch him when he jumped but let him hit the ground—my God you can't make this stuff up, but no. He opened his eyes and rolled his head a little toward me and said, woman I don't want to do another winter and I'm more than half crazy and now you've got a cancer in your head and you'll be just like me before long. At first it was like I had been hit with a fist in the stomach and I couldn't even say a word, but I looked at him—and this gets hard here I must admit—and he teared up and his nose started to run and I took a kleenex and mopped it. Then after a minute or so I suppose it was I said, well Pa I don't want to do another one either, and what's more, I don't want to do the radar or the poison. And I never went to a single appointment. They called me and called me for what seemed like a month but it was only several days I suppose and then they gave up, but not before threatening to get hold of you and make a stink. Well, I said, you people tell anyone—especially my children—a single personal detail about my health issues and I will drain my life savings on bulldog lawyers to chew on your asses. (I actually said that). That seemed to do it. I am sorry about the stories I told you on the phone. All said and done, I would have to say it was my cancer that really did it, because it was going to take me away from him and I don't trust some flunkies making $8 an hour in a nursing home that smells like pee to remember to set him in the sun, much less wipe his behind when he can't remember why he smells. (paragraph alert to the old coot)

Well, I should start on the <u>end</u> of the trip stuff—really confusing if you let yourself dwell on it for long, and we have. Mostly me, truth be told, since your father is long past deep thinking, but I know he would agree with me on what I'm about to ramble about. First, I refuse to use the S-word. If some 40 year old man who has lost his job, or some woman whose husband has run off with a tramp, if somebody like that does it, then yes, S-word. But look at us, for crying out loud. Past 80, with our brains (which is who we are) nearly rotted away. And what is left of them only wants to leave together, with a smidge of dignity? That is the S-word?? I can't imagine that. But—damn it, the dignity thing does bother me some because I think it is close to vanity, and you both know very well how I despised the vain people in this world. But then I think, come on here, vanity is how Gladys Stewart (70 if she is a day) keeps her hair coal black, or how Eldon Dummermuth (has to be close to 70) wears that silly gold dog chain snagged up in his white chest hair with his collar open in January. And that is all about looks and showing off. But our leaving early doesn't have a single thing to do with looks or showing off, for crying out loud, it has to do with not wanting to be considered worthless. Now don't get upset, we know very well that neither of you, or the grandkids, would ever consider us that. Anyway, I'm dropping that and that is the end of it. Dignity is OK but vanity is not, and we weren't being vain. And there is the practical side too, and even if we're not rich we do have some things and money we want you and your families to have and we can't bear the thought of hanging around until we have drained every last penny. That just seems downright silly the more I thought about it. And please, please, pretty please do <u>not</u> get carried away and spend thousands on planting us in some gold colored case with bells and whistles that looks like it might crank a jet engine and take off on its own. I can't believe that you would, since you can't miss the notes we signed and stapled to this letter which we <u>do</u> mean to be taped to our caskets even if does make the funeral home people mad. (paragraph alert before the grand final) Wait, one more little thing, or maybe it isn't. Please, please close the lids before the visitation and service. I can understand if you all want to look at our poor battered shells one last time, but anybody else, no way. It couldn't be for any healthy reason I can think of. Make that two more things. Our clothes are laid out on our bed, and don't you dare replace your father's old golf shirt with a dress shirt and tie. You know how much he hated those things. You've heard him say a hundred times how much he hoped the fool that invented ties died on the gallows.

OK, big breath here. The H words. I think I'll do this by elimination. You don't know this, but I have struggled my whole Christian life with Hell. You do know about my scars from the leaf fire when I was 7. I've never talked much about it, because I can't stand to. Believe it or not, the memories of the pain haunt me to this day. And you have to remember that back then out in the country was very different from how it would have gone today, or even when you were kids. Which brings me to my issue—I can't imagine what it would have been like if more than my arm and neck were burned, and in my worst nightmare I can't begin to consider <u>eternity</u> with my whole body being turned into a French fry that never gets done. I got off on this about 3 years ago and actually made myself sick to throwing up. I told your father it was bad mayo so I wouldn't have to try to explain it to him. And I assure you that me and your father have never wavered in our belief in God. And we know what the Bible says about Hell and we know the story of Lazarus calling back from Hell with his warning, but still, my God (I guess that is a prayer in a way) surely that is a parable. So—I am eliminating that possibility—Ha! as if <u>I</u> actually could. The only negative to the Heaven side of the deal is that I know we will be moved many streets down from Main Street by deciding not to accept all of our medicine—Ha! just realized that makes sense in two ways.

Well, I suppose that about covers it all. Your father and me are about to solve the great mystery and find out what only dead people know. If I forgot something, we can talk about it when you come to visit us at our little mansion in the back alley. I hope.

With great love and affection, Mom and Pa.

I'm frightfully in love with my wife, and would not do well without her. The words below flowed from me quickly. After beginning to tidy it all up with nice punctuation, I decided that such structured activity would serve no purpose. Some deeply soul-born thoughts are best left untidy, perhaps because the soul itself is so untidy.

HER

Ten days have passed in a blur and I wander seeking union with the dead I am Dylan's creature void of form I wander now over the landscape of our bedroom the soles of my bare feet inching over the floor seeking the places where her skin touched the varnished hardwood knowing that her oil is one with the varnish but fading and I resist the urge to lick the floor then I kneel at her side of the unmade bed to gently pull down the quilt and with my fingertips trace the scumbled outline of her body on the sheet my hands driven by their own engines find the pillow and cup the missing tangled black curls that I can feel as surely as I can feel the cool cloth I know then that I will not leave this room alive and I am comforted by the thought her nightgown and robe silky pink and fluffy white hang on a peg inside the bathroom door I have no memory of rising or leaving the bedside greedily I pull them together fill my hands with the blended cloth and bury my face I have done this a hundred times already and wept only the first time fearing that my tears would dilute her scent and this fear was stronger than my desire to shed them I drink it in like a starving man smelling steam rising from a rich broth the shotgun a tool long and black waits on its pegs inside the walk-in closet I imagine the dark hole of the muzzle disappearing as I tuck it beneath my chin careful to tilt the muzzle slightly rearward the barrel is in my left hand and with my right hand I reach down to locate the safety and flick it off with my thumb before it slips over the trigger I stare up at the grainy white sheetrock ceiling and visualize the softball-sized hole around which are scattered red flecks of skin and bone plastered together with chunks of hair my vision telescopic as the little chunks of flesh morph into red stalactites clinging tenaciously I am gliding toward the closet door now cannot feel the floor but know the landscape is real again the wave centers in my chest and its rising waters consume peacefully now an ocean sound still faraway in my head but it too will rise with the wave that will carry me to heaven or hell or someplace else that must be where we meet again maybe as children or wrinkled and ancient I care not which or where in between just let us meet I pause at the sounds rising with the ocean and listen closely and separate them and can hear little bird voices in an April morn and quick feet dancing over the living room floor and the chirping meaningless at first then comes the grandpa grandpa grandpa and I know that they have come to save me from death and to condemn me to life without her.